Lyla Lyte
and the
Li'berry Fruit

I'dreyah Ricketts

**Other books by
I'deyah Ricketts**

Lyla Lyte and the Loot Tree

Where Are the Animals?
(Children's Picture Book)

For more information about the author,
visit ideyahricketts.com.

Lyla Lyte
and the
Li'berry Fruit

by I'deyah Ricketts
illustrated by Katie Williams

Climbing Clouds Publishing
Chicago

Thank you for all of your support, influence,
and belief in me!

Mom and Dad

Baby brother, Josiah

Grandparents

Aunts and uncles

Friends

Cousins

Supporters

Favorite authors

South Loop family

Contents

1

Lost for Words

"I can't come up with the right words," Lyla Lyte mumbled as she sat at her desk staring at a blank white sheet of paper. "What is wrong with my brain?"

It was Thursday morning and everyone in Room 201 had finished their writing assignment with ease—everyone except nine-year-old Lyla. She sat there wanting her essay describing her hometown of Screenfield, Illinois, to come alive.

Tightly gripping her No. 2 pencil, Lyla wrote and then erased everything, trying hard to come up with colorful and spicy words, but her brain didn't respond. It was like she had a Do Not Use sign posted on her forehead.

"Here you go," whispered Lyla's best friend, Samantha Huggins, who had been watching Lyla fidget with her pencil like crazy. Samantha placed her completed essay on Lyla's desk. "Just copy mine."

Lyla and Samantha had been best friends since kindergarten. Looking out for one another was just one of the many qualities that made them like two peas in a pod. They were the same height, both taller than the other girls in fourth grade at Crinkle Academy, and they had the same round faces with cute baby bear noses. Their skin tone differed, with Lyla being a tad bit lighter. Both girls' hair was jet black, but Lyla's was much shorter than Samantha's. That day Lyla wore two orange scrunchies that hugged her puffs, while Samantha wore one white scrunchie wrapped around her long ponytail.

"No ... thank you," Lyla whispered politely, handing the essay back to Samantha. Then Lyla looked at the clock, and it seemed as though the second hand started moving rapidly. The time to complete her assignment was almost over.

She was determined to use her imagination but didn't know how, so she sat there struggling to come up with the right words. No matter how hard she tried, the words on the page were either too simple or simply boring! Lyla wasn't the only child in Screenfield who suffered from a lack of imagination. There were NO books in the town, and all of the children grew up without reading a single one.

They didn't even know that books existed, so they couldn't pretend to be superheroes, princes and princesses, football players, fairies, or cowboys and cowgirls, because they simply didn't know how. This made life boring for them.

The only outlet for the children in Screenfield was watching tubevision, and there were at least four of them for every person living in town. An outsider would assume that Screenfield's children were having a ball because they got to watch tubevision from sunup to sundown, but that was not the case.

Charles Crinkle, the mayor of Screenfield, only allowed ONE channel to be broadcasted on the tubevisions. That channel was called CrinkleTube,

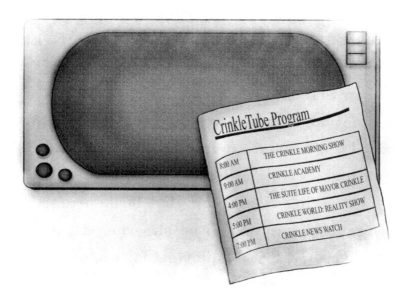

CrinkleTube Program

8:00 AM	THE CRINKLE MORNING SHOW
9:00 AM	CRINKLE ACADEMY
4:00 PM	THE SUITE LIFE OF MAYOR CRINKLE
5:00 PM	CRINKLE WORLD: REALITY SHOW
7:00 PM	CRINKLE NEWS WATCH

named after him, of course. Any Screenfield citizen wanting a program of their own on CrinkleTube had to apply for a permit, which Mayor Crinkle always denied.

Watching CrinkleTube was like being tortured. The mayor served as the network's only host, guest, actor, and news reporter. CrinkleTube's program schedule was exactly the same every single day, week, month, and year.

Mayor Crinkle worked and lived in City Hall, a huge building the size of a mansion that sat on top of Knob Hill, west of downtown Screenfield. This is where he placed the huge antenna he built that sent the signal to everyone's tubevision.

"Please pass your papers to the front, everyone," instructed Ms. Verdak. She was the Classroom Tube Assistant (CTA) for Room 201, one of the many assistants assigned to help the Tube Teacher. Not surprisingly, Mayor Crinkle was Crinkle Academy's only Tube Teacher. He was also the principal. Instead of books, children learned from a forty-inch tubevision, which sat in front of all the classes.

Ms. Verdak usually wore long, pretty, silk skirts and short-sleeve blouses that complimented her petite frame. She was extremely pleasant, unlike the Tube Teacher, and she always wore her hair in golden brown braids that dropped past her shoulders. Lyla thought Ms. Verdak was a lot younger than her mom, but she wouldn't dare ask her age. Children just didn't do things like that.

As Lyla sat trying to add words to make her assignment unique, her classmates walked past her desk to turn in their essays. She assumed they wrote the same five descriptive answers on their papers as she normally did on her own.

Soon, all of Lyla's classmates' papers were stacked in a neat pile on Ms. Verdak's desk. Mary Englemouth, who sat to the left of Lyla, suddenly raised her hand. If she had known the word *blabbermouth* actually existed, Lyla would probably have told Mary that Blabbermouth, not Englemouth, should be her last name. Mary couldn't keep her mouth shut for anything, and she told Ms. Verdak about everything and everyone in the class. At the top of Mary Englemouth's list of classmates to pester was Lyla.

Lyla could never understand how a girl who always wore pretty dresses with BIG bows could be such a bully. Maybe Mary Englemouth didn't like the oversized bows, or how her mom cluttered her strawberry-colored hair with all types of funny-looking trinkets, so she took her resentment out on Lyla.

"Yes, Mary?" Ms. Verdak asked.

"Lyla still has her assignment," tattled Mary.

Ms. Verdak looked at Lyla and saw only the top of her head because she was focused on the paper on her desk. "Lyla, why are you taking such a long time to complete the writing assignment?" she asked, concerned. "You're the only one who didn't turn it in."

"I'm **Lost for Words**!" answered Lyla, gradually picking up her sad, round face.

"You'd better find them!" taunted Mary Englemouth. Some of the classmates couldn't help but giggle.

"OK, class ... you know that's not nice," said Ms. Verdak. "Lyla, you have five minutes to finish, so please hurry up."

Lyla still tried and tried to come up with rich, descriptive words. She could have been like everyone else and written a two-sentence essay, but she didn't want to. She wanted very badly to make her paper stand out. So, she sat there thinking like a bird unable to fly ... a tree unable to grow ... a pencil unable to write.

For a brief moment, Lyla gazed at the tubevision on the cart positioned in front of the class. *I hate learning from that thing,* she thought. *Learning should be fun. If only that tubevision could break.* Lyla wanted change for Screenfield. She was tired of CrinkleTube. Deep in her heart, she knew there was much more to life than watching boring tubevision.

When Lyla's time elapsed, Ms. Verdak pointed to the circular, white clock on the wall and said, "Lyla, your time is up. Please bring me your essay."

She stood and slowly approached Ms. Verdak's desk. "Here you go," she said quietly.

Only her full name, Lyla Lyte, was on the paper (in the top left corner, of course).

"Lyla, you didn't write anything," Ms. Verdak said as she flipped Lyla's paper over to see if she had written anything on the back. Then she looked at Lyla and said regretfully, "I'm sorry … but I have to give you an *F*."

"Oh no!" Lyla exclaimed. "My mom and dad are going to be upset."

"Lyla, you are a great student, but I have no other choice. You took way too long to finish."

"Can you give me more time, please?" asked Lyla. "And … Did I tell you that I like your pretty high-heel shoes. They go well with your beautiful outfit. Are they new?"

"I will not give you more time!" replied Ms. Verdak. "It wouldn't be fair to the other students … and, yes, my shoes are new … thank you." Then Ms. Verdak took her fat, red marker and wrote a gigantic, red *F* across Lyla's entire paper.

"Ooouuu!" sounded the whole class. Everyone was stunned.

Lyla had just made history. She was now the first student to receive an *F* on a writing assignment at Crinkle Academy.

"Lyla, I want this paper returned tomorrow with a parent's signature," Ms. Verdak said sternly. "If you don't bring it to school tomorrow, I will have to call your parents in for a Parent Conference."

"Shoot!" Lyla moaned as she slowly turned to face the class.

All eyes were locked on her. Even though the other students already knew, Lyla still tried to cover up the red *F* on her paper. Walking back to her desk was going to be brutal, probably the hardest thing she would ever have to do in her entire life. She felt sick in her tummy with embarrassment, and her cheeks flushed red hot.

She could not help but look at Mary Englemouth, whose thin, pink lips mouthed "Dummy" over and over again.

For a moment, Lyla considered running full blast out of Room 201 ... out of the school ... straight to her house ... underneath her bed covers ... and not coming out until next spring. But she didn't.

This is the WORST day of my life! Lyla thought as she took the first step toward her seat.

2

Life Before Tubevision

After school, Lyla was not in a hurry to get home. She was petrified by what was in store for her when her parents saw the dreaded grade. Accompanied by her best friends—Samantha, Nick Nelson, and Megan Heinz, or the Troops, as they called themselves—she took the extra-long route home. Along the way, they passed Crinkle Cuts, Dish Dining, and The Tulip Emporium, some of Screenfield's most popular stores.

When they finally arrived at Lyla's house, the Troops formed a circle around Lyla and gave her the biggest, most supportive group hug. It was quite obvious that Lyla had grown more and more nervous since Ms. Verdak wrote the *F* on her paper.

"Do you want us to go inside with you?" asked Samantha.

Megan swung open the gate. "Yeah! You might need us."

"No," responded Lyla. "I'll be all right."

"Are you sure?" Nick asked.

"I'm sure," responded Lyla. "You guys didn't get the bad grade. I did. Thank you, Troops, but I must do this all by myself."

That was one of Lyla's most unique qualities. When she messed up, she owned up to it and faced the consequences, no matter what. This time was no different. She composed herself, waved good-bye for the tenth time, and then turned to go inside to face her mom.

Lyla moped into the house, took off her shoes, and placed them on the gray, ceramic tile in the foyer. Mrs. Lyte was preparing Lyla's favorite after-school snacks: homemade chocolate chip cookies, sliced cucumbers with fresh lime, and warm soy milk. The smell of the baking sweets filled the air, but it did nothing to help reduce Lyla's anxiety.

"Lyla, is that you?" Mrs. Lyte asked loudly.

"Yes, it is," she responded in a low voice.

Mrs. Lyte sensed something was wrong the moment she heard her daughter's raspy voice. She entered the foyer wearing her pine green apron with bright yellow tulips printed on the front. She treasured her garden of beautiful wild tulips. She loved them so much that almost every piece of clothing she owned had tulips on them,

14

even her socks. She always wore her hair in a bun, and every morning she picked a fresh tulip from the garden and placed it in her hair.

"What's wrong? Did something bad happen at school today?" her mom asked.

Without answering, Lyla handed her mom the piece of paper.

"What is this *F* for? There's nothing on your paper," her mom said while adjusting her eyes to the horrific grade.

"I didn't finish my writing assignment," Lyla explained. "So ... Ms. Verdak gave me an *F* and you have to sign it."

"You never had difficulty writing before," Mrs. Lyte said, still confused by the *F* on her daughter's paper.

Lyla agreed. "I know, but this time I wanted to make my assignment different from my classmates'. I didn't want to write the same boring essay as everyone else." Her eyes filled with tears, and she made her best crybaby face.

"Hush ... don't cry," her mom said while rubbing Lyla's shoulder.

"I'm nothing but a dummy," exclaimed Lyla.

"You're not a dummy," her mom promptly responded.

"So why can't I use my imagination to write?" asked Lyla in a crybaby voice that matched her facial expression.

Mrs. Lyte did not have an answer, so instead she gave her daughter a big hug.

After a couple of moments, Lyla's mood dimmed again when she remembered her *F*.

"Sooo ... What's my punishment?" Lyla asked.

"Nothing," her mom said, shaking her head. "Getting that *F* is punishment enough."

Lyla looked at her mom in disbelief and wiped away the tears that had formed in the corners of her eyes. She couldn't believe she wasn't going to be punished.

"Why don't you go watch *The Suite Life of Mayor Crinkle?*" she suggested. "It will make you feel better."

"Boring, boring, boring!" Lyla complained and folded her arms. "I would rather babysit my annoying baby brother than watch *The Suite Life of Mayor Crinkle.*"

Then she walked away, bypassing the thirty-two-inch tubevision that sat on a stubby, glass stand in the living room. Lyla stopped at the window and pushed the ruffled, beige curtains aside.

Mrs. Lyte stood there watching Lyla for a few moments. She couldn't bear to see the reflection of her daughter's big, brown, gloomy eyes in the square-framed picture window. She felt compelled to tell her something that would lift her spirits. She walked over to her daughter and said, "I shouldn't be telling you this, but—"

"Telling me what?" Lyla interrupted, turning to give her mom her undivided attention.

"There used to be something in Screenfield called books," her mom began.

"What's a book?" Lyla asked, filled with curiosity.

"A book is a set of pages with printed words held together between a protective cover on the front and back," answered her mom. "And sometimes they're filled with colorful pictures. A book teaches you how to do new things. The best thing about a book is that it takes you on amazing adventures without you having to leave your seat."

Lyla was baffled. "How could a book take you on an adventure?"

"Because you use your imagination as you read," her mom responded while pointing to Lyla's head. "The more you read, the more your imagination G-R-O-W-S!"

Lyla started to forget all about the dreadful grade she received as she listened to her mom's description of books.

"Sooo … What happened to all the books in Screenfield?" she asked.

Lyla's mom sat down in the family's wooden rocking chair, which creaked under her weight, and looked at her daughter, who sat on the plush, tan carpet.

Lyla's mom began telling her a story of **Life Before Tubevision**. "It goes far back to when your dad and I were teenagers ... before the town was actually named Screenfield."

"What was it called?" asked Lyla.

"Coverfield," answered her mom.

"Like a cover on a book?" Lyla said, remembering the vivid description of books her mom had just given her.

"Yes," her mom replied and nodded. "In fact, reading was more popular than anything else. You couldn't catch a person, young or old, without a book in his or her hand. Children had loads of fun reading because the books gave them opportunities for their creative imaginations to run wild."

"Wild!" Lyla repeated. "How can a child's imagination go wild?"

Mrs. Lyte pointed to her own head this time. "There was no limit to where they could go when they used their imaginations."

"Wowww!" exclaimed Lyla, smiling. "How did all that change?" she inquired, shrugging her shoulders.

"One sunny morning, a pudgy stranger with a bald head, a bushy, black mustache, and florescent purple eyeglasses drove into town," said Lyla's mom. "He had this crazy-looking machine in the bed of his pickup truck."

"It was Mayor Crinkle!" she blurted excitedly. Even her nineteen-month-old brother, Joey, could have figured that out. "When you mentioned his shiny head, I just knew that was who you were talking about."

"You're correct," her mom said, nodding.

"What was the crazy thingamabob he had?" asked Lyla.

"A tubevision," her mom said while pointing to the one they had sitting in the living room.

"So *that's* where it came from," Lyla said.

Mrs. Lyte continued, "He told the townspeople that he invented it, and that it would make our lives more exciting and enjoyable. The old mayor directed him straight to City Hall so he could present it to everyone."

"The old mayor?" Lyla sounded surprised. "Who was the mayor when you and Dad were teenagers?"

"Mayor Richard Goodman," her mom said as she placed her hand over her heart and closed her eyes, remembering the past. For a few seconds, Mrs. Lyte reminisced about how kind and fair Mayor Goodman was to the people of Coverfield.

"Did people go to City Hall to see what it was?" Lyla asked, interrupting her mother's trip down memory lane.

"Everyone in town was curious to see what this tubevision was all about. But when *Mister*

21

Crinkle, as he was known back then, plugged the tubevision in, nothing but a blank screen stared back at us," she explained, shaking her head. "The townspeople took him for a fool and everyone laughed at him."

Lyla sighed softly. She remembered how she felt standing in front of class with the *F* on her paper, and how embarrassed she was when Mary Englemouth made fun of her. Hearing about how the townspeople laughed at Mayor Crinkle made her feel a smidge of compassion for him. "Poor man. Did Mayor Goodman kick him out of town?" she asked sorrowfully.

"No," her mom answered. "Mayor Goodman felt so sorry for him that he hired Mr. Crinkle as his assistant."

"Sounds like Mayor Goodman was a good mayor," commented Lyla.

"He sure was!" she said, grinning from ear to ear at the memory. "He was the best mayor we ever had."

"Why isn't Mayor Goodman still the mayor? Why did he quit?" Lyla asked.

Her mom paused. "He didn't. Mayor Goodman passed away, and then Mr. Crinkle took control of the mayor's office and became very powerful. He eventually figured out that the tubevision didn't work because there was no broadcasting signal in town."

"Is that when he built that gigantic antenna on top of City Hall?" Lyla asked, her eyes bulging. "That thing is huge!"

"Yes, that's when he built the antenna," replied her mom. "We wouldn't be able to watch tubevision without it."

"Not being able to watch tubevision," cheered Lyla, "would be a good thing!"

"Now, Lyla! Without tubevision your dad would not have a job," her mom said, interrupting Lyla's happy moment.

Mr. Lyte was tubevision's camera operator. He was responsible for taping all of the programs on CrinkleTube. Her father had worked at City Hall for twenty-five years and was Mayor Crinkle's most loyal employee.

"I know," said Lyla, her smile flipping upside

down. "I wouldn't want that to happen."

"Do you know that Mayor Crinkle knows who is watching tubevision?" Lyla's mom asked.

"He can look at us as we watch ours?" asked Lyla.

She quickly stood, ran to the tubevision, and turned it on. Lyla looked straight into the screen and yelled, "Hello, Mayor Crinkle! Can you see me doing this?" She began jumping up and down with her hands fluttering above her head.

Mrs. Lyte cracked up. "Not like that, silly. Come back over here so I can explain," she ordered, still laughing at her daughter's silly antics. Lyla sat back on the carpet, breathing hard from jumping.

"He always knows how many people are watching because he placed a tiny viewer-rating device in every tubevision. That device lets him know instantly who has their tubevision on or off," Mrs. Lyte explained.

"Ohhh!" said Lyla. "That's how."

"When he first broadcasted CrinkleTube, the viewer-rating devices told him that no one was watching," her mom explained. "Rather than watch, everyone chose to read books. After a few months, Mayor Crinkle became furious!"

Lyla raised her eyebrows. "What did he do?"

"Mayor Crinkle ordered us to turn in all of our books. Loads of people brought all types of books to City Hall, but the mayor didn't stop there. He went to every home, school, and library, forcing us to turn in every single book in town."

"What was a li'berry?" Lyla asked. "It sounds like the name of a fruit."

Her mom chuckled. "The word is pronounced *library*," she said, correcting her daughter. "And, no, you don't eat it."

"So ... What was it?" asked Lyla.

"A *library* is a huge building with thousands of books on every subject that you can think of," answered her mom. "Our library was located at the bottom of Knob Hill. Inside were comfortable chairs for anyone to sit and read for hours. You could even borrow books and take them home to read."

"That sounds like the best ever," exclaimed

Lyla. "What happened to the li'berry? *Oops*! I mean, *library*."

Mrs. Lyte paused for a second, and then said, "Mayor Crinkle demolished it."

"De-mol-ished?" It was obvious Lyla didn't have a clue of what the word meant.

"He tore it down," her mom said.

Lyla became upset. "He shouldn't have done a horrible thing like that. We should get him to build another library in Screenfield," she said angrily.

"That dream will never come true," her mom responded.

"Dream?" Lyla said. "What do you mean by dream?"

"A dream is something you want to happen so much that you work hard to make it happen," explained her mom.

Suddenly, Joey woke up and began bawling loudly. Her mom politely excused herself to hurry upstairs to get him. Lyla thought Joey was extremely annoying, and that his bald head was too big for his little brown body. In fact, she believed his big head was the reason he fell all the time. He already had at least four tiny dents on his head (which she had just counted the past week). Lyla believed Joey always interrupted great conversations she had with her mom, and this day was no exception. Stuff like this aggravated Lyla.

Her mom returned moments later with Joey in her arms. She held him in the crook of her arm. He was wearing a purple, one-piece outfit. In her mother's free hand was an old, black-and-white picture. From the fold marks, Lyla knew the picture must have been taken before she was born. As soon as her mom sat back down, she said, "This is a picture of my mom sitting in this very rocking chair reading a children's picture book to me. I was about Joey's age when the picture was taken."

Before Lyla could take a look, Joey reached out, grabbed the picture, and tried to put it in his mouth (babies literally try to eat everything). The picture ripped into two equivalent pieces. Joey held one half, and Lyla's mom held the other.

"JOEYYY!" Mrs. Lyte yelled as she jumped up.

"You should have left him in his crib," Lyla said angrily.

"Lyla, leave him alone," her mom ordered as she placed Joey down on the carpet in front of the tubevision. Then she snatched the torn half of the picture out of his little baby hand. She sat down and took the two pieces and fit them together like a jigsaw puzzle.

"All I need is a little tape to fix it," she said as she placed the adhesive on the back of each half of the picture. Once she was done, she flipped it over and pointed to a spot in the picture. "This," she said, "is how a book looks."

"Amazing!" Lyla exclaimed. She was astonished by the look of it, but at the same time surprised by how simple it looked. She thought that something so valuable would be covered in diamonds and gold, but it was not. "What did Mayor Crinkle do with all the books when he collected them?" she asked.

"One night, he enforced a curfew—" she began, before Lyla interrupted.

Lyla poked herself in the chest with her thumb. "Like my curfew?"

"Yes, but this was for everyone in town," replied her mom. "We had to be in the house by 10:00 p.m. and could not come back outside until 7:00 a.m. the next morning. During the curfew, he buried the books deep down in the ground."

Lyla quickly stood up and asked, "Where?"

"No one knows," her mom answered. "It happened such a long time ago."

"You have to know something!" exclaimed Lyla.

Her mom thought for a moment. "Well, I did hear once that the books were buried east of downtown Screenfield."

Lyla became hyped up with excitement. *If I find those books, it could help not only me use my imagination, but all of the children in Screenfield,* she thought to herself. She couldn't wait to deliver the good news to the Troops. "I have to tell Samantha, Megan, and Nick about the buried books tomorrow," she said with excitement.

"No!" shouted Lyla's mom as she leaped out of the rocking chair. She startled Lyla and Joey, who had managed to stand up in front of the tubevision while his mother and sister were talking. His mother's loud "NO" caused him to lose his balance and fall, head first, onto the plush living room carpet (dent number five). He instantly began to bawl, and greenish snot dripped from his nose. Their mom rushed to pick him up.

"Don't tell anyone about this story!" she demanded.

"Why?" asked Lyla, confused.

"It must remain our secret," replied her mom. "Everyone in town has forgotten about books. We don't want to give any of your friends the idea that there is something better than tubevision," she explained gravely. "If Mayor Crinkle finds out that we are spreading news about books, he will fire your dad and throw us all in that atrocious jail!"

"What does a-tro-cious mean?" asked Lyla.

Her mom shook her head. "You don't want to know!"

Her mom's reluctance to define the word made Lyla think jail was a cruel and chilling place. She loved her precious freedom too much for it to be snatched away. On top of that, she knew her dad truly cherished his job. He would be devastated if he were fired, and doubly so if she was the reason why he was fired. So, even though she wanted to tell the Troops, she decided to keep the story about books to herself.

"I won't tell anyone. I swear," Lyla promised while crossing her two slender pinky fingers.

"I believe you," her mom said as she gave Lyla a half hug with one arm, while holding Joey with the other. "Now, go watch some CrinkleTube."

"I said it was boring!" responded Lyla. She didn't budge.

3

Keeping a Secret
a Secret

The next morning, while eating breakfast in her white T-shirt, orange shorts, and white, knee-high socks, all Lyla could think about was the story of the buried books. She even cut her pancakes into small squares to resemble the book in the photograph her mother had shown her the night before. After breakfast, Lyla grabbed her cinch sack and stood by the front door to wait for her dad, who took her to school each morning. Half of the time, she was tardy because he took so much time to get ready in the morning.

"Here's your lunch," Mrs. Lyte said.

That morning Mrs. Lyte wore her pine green robe with printed yellow tulips and matching house shoes. She handed Lyla a brown paper bag. Inside was the usual: turkey sandwich on wheat bread, sliced apples, Crinkle Lemonade juice box, and chocolate chip cookies.

"Thanks, Mom," said Lyla.

"Have a nice day. And remember ... Shhh about our secret!" Mrs. Lyte said, placing her finger against her full, shaded lips.

At that moment, Lyla's dad bolted down the stairs while still tying his gray tie. He always dressed the same for work: a neatly pressed black suit, a white collared shirt, tie, and black slip-on dress shoes.

"Honey, your lunch and coffee are on the kitchen counter," said Mrs. Lyte. She had put leftover pizza from last night's dinner in a container, and filled his favorite travel mug with steaming coffee.

Mr. Lyte loved that his wife took a leave of absence from her job as the manager of The Tulip Emporium (where they grew and sold an assortment of tulips) to be a stay-at-home mom. Even though Mrs. Lyte loved staying home to care for her family, she looked forward to returning to work.

"Lyla, it's time to go," her dad said.

He grabbed his lunch, briefcase, car keys, and coffee, and then turned to walk toward his daughter waiting at the front door.

"Good-bye," her mom said before kissing both of them on their cheeks.

After Lyla and her dad got into the family van, they strapped on their seatbelts and drove off. Lyla began their morning-drive-to-school conversation with an interesting question: "Dad, do grown-ups like Mayor Crinkle?"

"Some people do, some people don't," he answered with his eyes still locked on the road.

"Do you like him?" Lyla asked.

"He's my boss," answered her dad, who had taken advantage of the red traffic light to take a cautious sip of his coffee.

"Sooo … you have to like him?" asked Lyla, looking at the reflection of her father's eyes in the rearview mirror.

"Too many questions this morning," replied Mr. Lyte. "Can we talk about something else, Lyla?"

Although she heard her dad's request, she needed to ask just one more question to satisfy her mind. So, she silently built up enough courage, and then asked, "Would you quit your job if you could?"

Mr. Lyte abruptly pulled over to the side of

the road and slammed on the breaks. When the van came to a sudden stop, he spilled coffee all over his dress slacks. "Oouuch!" he yelled.

"Dad, are you OK?" Lyla asked as she swiftly poked her head between the front seats.

I'm all right," he replied as he shifted the van into park, opened the glove compartment, and pulled out napkins to clean up the mess. "Why would I quit my job?"

"I just wanted to ask," Lyla said hesitantly. "She enjoyed the morning conversations with her father and was a little afraid that, because of her question, he might not want to talk anymore.

Mr. Lyte realized that his daughter was only being a typical nine-year-old. He turned to Lyla in the backseat and said, "Lyla, I love my job too much to just leave. What else would I do in Screenfield?"

Lyla didn't have an answer. "I don't know," she said softly as she shrugged her shoulders and slouched down in the backseat.

"Well, let's get you to school," her dad said, "before it gets even later."

He turned around to face the front, shifted the gear into drive and sped off. Lyla didn't bother asking her dad any more questions the rest of the ride to school.

As Lyla hopped out of the family van, she decided that day at school was going to be utterly different from the day before. Even though the episode with her dad didn't go as planned, it didn't ruin her morning. Lyla still felt like a VIP (Very Important Person) because she was the only child in Screenfield that knew the story of the buried books. She had a Big Secret.

Lyla waved good-bye to her dad as he drove off, and then turned toward the steel double-entry doors of Crinkle Academy. *I wonder what the name of the school was before Mister Crinkle became mayor*, she thought as she strolled past the life-size, bronze statue of Mayor Crinkle holding a small fifteen-inch tubevision. All of the

CTAs made sure the statue remained spotless. That was part of their daily duties. Lyla looked around the schoolyard to see if anyone was around. When she realized the coast was clear, she quickly kicked dirt onto the foot of the statue and then scurried off to class.

Class was about to begin when Lyla entered Room 201. Greeting her was a wall filled with her classmates' essays. Bright red *A*s were written on each one, except her own. Lyla's paper was tucked neatly away in the yellow folder she placed in her drawstring cinch sack.

"Good morning, Lyla," Ms. Verdak said from her desk. She was preparing for the morning lesson while she waited for all of her students to arrive.

"Hi," Lyla responded.

Suddenly, Mary Englemouth rushed past Lyla, purposely bumping into her, to give Ms. Verdak a shiny red apple.

"This apple was grown especially for you," said Mary Englemouth, glancing at Lyla with a devilish look. "It was the best apple out of the bunch."

Lyla didn't know which was sweeter: the apple or Mary Englemouth's sweet-talking.

"Thank you, Mary," Ms. Verdak said, placing the apple atop a stack of papers.

"You're very welcome," Mary Englemouth said loud enough for the entire class to hear her.

When she turned to go back to her seat, she covered the side of her mouth so Ms. Verdak couldn't see and stuck her tongue out at Lyla. She gave Lyla another sly bump, then walked back to her desk.

I'm not going to let her ruin my morning, Lyla thought.

"Before you take your seat, Lyla, do you have something for me?" Ms. Verdak asked and held her hand out palm up.

Lyla opened her cinch sack and retrieved her dreadfully graded assignment from the day before.

Her mom's curly signature was at the bottom in dark blue ink. "Here you go," Lyla said as she handed the paper to Ms. Verdak.

40

"Thank you! You can take your seat now," Ms. Verdak instructed.

As Lyla turned and squeezed past Mary Englemouth's desk, she heard her say, "Dummy!" but Lyla ignored it entirely.

"I know you heard me," Mary whispered. Lyla continued to ignore Mary's attempts to make her angry. She had something more important on her mind than being preoccupied with her rival's antics.

Ms. Verdak stood and walked around her desk. "The first subject of the day will be science," she said before turning on the tubevision.

Mayor Crinkle, with his shiny, bald head, suddenly appeared on the screen. He was dressed in a bright red suit with a black, collared shirt and black silk tie. In the background was a sign sitting on an easel with Crinkle Academy's slogan: "The Best Student is a Crinkle Student."

Like every other morning, Mayor Crinkle threw on his purple florescent eyeglasses and greeted all of the students with his song:

♩

Good morning, good morning,
good morning to you.
Good morning, good morning,
and how do you do?
This morning, this morning,
we're all in our places.

This morning, this morning,
with sun-shining faces.
Each morning, each morning,
we come happy to school.

Each morning, each morning,
'cause your Tube Teacher is cool.
This is the way, this is the way
we start our Crinkle Academy day!
Ohhh yeahhh!

♩

During the atrocious singing, the majority of the class shouted, "BOO, BOO, BOO!"

"Class, that's enough," Ms. Verdak shouted angrily.

"But he sings horribly," said a student named Jonny Knocks, still covering his ears. He was the biggest student in Room 201.

"Johnny, stop being rude," demanded Ms. Verdak, pointing at him.

When the howling ended, Mayor Crinkle said, "Hi, students! Are you ready to have the best school day in Screenfield?"

Johnny cried out again, "It's going to be the worst day!"

"JOHNYYY!" bellowed Ms. Verdak. "Do you want to have silent lunch?"

"No," Johnny said softly as he began to slowly sink down in his seat.

Lyla couldn't get the buried books off her mind. It was becoming more and more difficult to **Keep a Secret ... a Secret**. She wanted so badly to tell the Troops, but she knew her mother would be upset if she found out Lyla had told anyone about the books. *But Samantha, Megan, and Nick are not just anyone*, Lyla thought. *They are my best, best, best friends.*

Finally, after going back and forth in her mind, Lyla made her decision. She got Samantha's attention by kicking her lightly on the side of her left sneaker, with its fat, white shoestrings.

Samantha leaned slightly and moved her left ear in Lyla's direction. "What?" she whispered, making sure to keep her eyeballs forward.

"I have a big secret," Lyla whispered back.

Samantha loved a good secret, as long as it wasn't about her. "What is it?" she asked enthusiastically, moving her ear closer.

"I'll only tell you and the other Troops," said Lyla.

"OK, but when?" Samantha asked, anxious to find out what Lyla's secret was. Samantha was always impatient.

"Since we're studying Screenfield's favorite plant this month," Mayor Crinkle said while adjusting his glasses, "your homework for the next seven weeks will be to plant a tulip bulb and watch it germinate."

"We don't know what that word means!" said Johnny.

"Yeah!" echoed the whole class. They supported Johnny like he was the chosen leader of Room 201.

"For those of you who don't know what the word *germinate* means," continued Mayor Crinkle, who must have heard the kids through the tubevision, "it means 'to grow' ... and it's spelled g-e-r-m-i-n-a-t-e."

"Class!" Ms. Verdak said sternly while tapping on her desk to get everyone's attention. "Make sure you all write that word and the definition on your papers."

Mayor Crinkle continued, "I want everyone to observe their seeds each week. At the end of the seventh week, each student will have to stand in front of the class and discuss your observations."

"I'll tell you guys when we go outside," Lyla responded. "Meet me by the monkey ba—"

Before Lyla could finish, Mary Englemouth's hand flew up in the air. "Ms. Verdak! Lyla is talking while Mayor Crinkle is teaching."

The whole class turned to stare at Lyla.

"Lyla!" Ms. Verdak said. "Pay attention to the tubevision."

"OK," she said, embarrassed because every-one's eyes were locked on her.

"Ha, ha, ha!" heckled Mary Englemouth, thinking it was hilarious. "You got in trouble … you got in trouble!"

Lyla just rolled her eyes, then directed her

attention back to the tubevision.

She was still scared to take on another writing assignment. "I'm glad we don't have to write down our observations, because I would get another *F*!" she mumbled to herself.

Mayor Crinkle lectured for the next forty-five minutes about the first plant he grew. Lyla's eyes were glued to the clock. As she watched the second hand make its way around the clock, she felt like she was going to explode with excitement. She couldn't wait to tell the Troops about the buried books.

4

Tree House

"**D**on't tell anyone what I'm about to tell you," warned Lyla as she looked around to see if anyone, namely Mary Englemouth, was listening. The Troops had gathered beneath the rusty blue monkey bars on the school playground to hear the big secret.

"You can trust us, Lyla," said Megan, even though she had a habit of telling people's secrets that they specifically asked her not to tell. Megan was the only girl with freckles at Crinkle Academy, and her blond hair was filled with bouncy curls.

"Mayor Crinkle buried something called books east of downtown Screenfield," Lyla whispered to her friends.

Samantha raised her hand as if she were still in class. "What are books?"

"You read them," answered Lyla. "And they help you learn new stuff. The best thing about books is that you can use your imagination when you read. The more you read, the better your imagination will get."

"I don't think that's possible," contested Nick. He was the only male member of the Troops, and he was a lot taller than Lyla, Samantha, and Megan. He had a caramel-candy complexion, and his hair was cut in a low Afro. Nick was one of the most handsome boys at Crinkle Academy, and he didn't know that Megan had the biggest crush on him. But, unlike Megan, who agreed with Nick's every word, Lyla and Nick battled like cats and dogs.

"Why don't you think using your imagination is possible?" Lyla asked, automatically annoyed by Nick's comment.

"You told us," reminded Nick, "that you got an *F* on your writing assignment because you tried to use your imagination."

Lyla promptly defended herself. "I got an *F* because we don't read books. All we do is watch tubevision *all ... day ... long.*"

"Because there's *nothing ... else ... to ... do!*" Nick declared.

"So we should just be happy with living a boring life?" asked Lyla, stepping closer to Nick with her hands on her hips. Her puffs swung in the wind as she bobbed her head back and forth.

Nick shoved his face forward. "I guess so!"

"Well, I'm not," rebutted Lyla. "And I'm going to do something about it."

After a few rounds, Samantha, the Troops' peacemaker, couldn't take it anymore. She was the one who always intervened to stop Lyla and Nick from squabbling. This time was no different. She stepped between the dueling duo and said, "Will you both just SHUT UP!"

Lyla and Nick stopped arguing instantly and retreated to their corners. Each of them folded their arms and pouted.

"Can we just hear more about the books?" Samantha asked, turning toward Lyla.

"OK!" Lyla said. "With books, you can go on adventures in your mind just by reading. My mom told me there used to be thousands of them with colorful pictures in Screenfield. Everyone read, even children like us."

"That's awesome," Samantha said, smiling at the thought of the news Lyla shared with them.

Megan was more skeptical. She wanted proof. "Show us one of those books you're talking about," she said, holding out her hand.

Lyla used all of her strength to slap the palm of Megan's hand.

"Ouch!" Megan yelped. She pulled her hand back and shook it so hard and fast that her fingers flapped against each other. "What was that for?" she asked, looking at Lyla with a frown.

Lyla pulled on Megan's earlobe. "Do you have something in your ears?" she asked. "I said the books were buried!"

"Oops ... sorry," Megan said while pulling her ear out of Lyla's grip.

"My mom told me," Lyla continued, making eye contact with everyone, "that the books were kept in a big place called a library—"

"What's a li'berry?" asked Nick, interrupting Lyla's story. "I've never heard of that word."

"It's *library*, not li'berry," Lyla said, correcting him as her mother had corrected her.

Nick stomped the ground with his high-top sneaker. "That's what I said ... *li'berry!*"

"You're saying it wrong!" declared Lyla.

"You're hearing it wrong!" disputed Nick.

"No, I heard you say *lie—bear—eee*," Lyla slowly repeated, breaking the word into three syllables.

At times like these, even Samantha couldn't stop them from quarrelling. The two fussed until Ms. Verdak instructed the class to line up.

"Everybody!" Lyla quickly said as they all ran to get in line. "Just meet me at my **Tree House** tomorrow at noon."

"GREAT!" Samantha and Megan replied. Nick just grunted, but Lyla knew his nonverbal gesture meant that he was still going to show up.

How dare he fuss with me! I know he said it wrong, thought Lyla as she marched back to class behind Nick. *I'm tired of him always trying to be right.* "See, Nick, you wasted all of our time!" Lyla whispered.

Nick couldn't believe Lyla was going to keep it up. He turned and whispered back heatedly, "No … You did!"

"I didn't!" Lyla said through clenched teeth. "You did!"

"No, it was you!" whispered Nick, pointing to

Lyla over his shoulder with his thumb.

As usual, Mary Englemouth was in the front of the line on the lookout for students not following the rules. As soon as she saw Lyla and Nick fussing, she immediately tapped Ms. Verdak on the back of her red, short-sleeve blouse and said, "Ms. Verdak, Lyla and Nick are talking in line."

Ms. Verdak turned around quickly. When her green eyes zeroed in on the two classmates, they pointed at each other and said, "He/she started it!"

It was exactly twelve o'clock when the Troops arrived at Lyla's house. They loved going there for two reasons: because her mom always baked the best chocolate chip cookies, which they couldn't wait to get their hands on, and because Lyla had a massive tree house in her backyard.

The tree house was ten feet high and looked like a small house suspended in the oak tree. It even had an arched roof with shingles. Her dad had nailed five pieces of plywood to the trunk of the tree so the Troops could climb up onto the wooden, porch-like platform and enter through the child-sized door.

Lyla's dad crafted a wooden shelf, where a nineteen-inch tubevision sat, and then ran a long, orange extension cord from the tubevision to an electrical outlet inside the house. It was the first tubevision Mayor Crinkle had in his fancy office. When he upgraded to a much larger one, he gave the old one to Lyla's dad (right after the knobs had fallen off). The picture on the tubevision was fuzzy, but it didn't matter because the Troops never turned it on.

Along with the tubevision, the tree house was decorated with a small, round, wooden table and four small, wooden chairs, one for each of the Troops.

"Hi, Mrs. Lyte," said the Troops, greeting her politely as they headed to the kitchen for cookies and soy milk.

"Make sure you all clean up your mess when you are done eating," instructed Lyla's mom.

"We will," everyone said.

"To the tree house," Lyla said enthusiastically as she headed out the door before everyone else. "And don't forget your cookies!"

"You don't have to worry about that," said Nick, his hands filled with cookies. He was the last one to exit the kitchen.

One by one, they all climbed up to the tree house, sat outside for a while, and then headed inside.

"OK, Troops, let's start planning." Lyla directed them to sit around the wooden table. "There are books buried somewhere out there, and we need to find them."

A worried expression spread across Nick's face as he bit into a cookie. "Do you guys think it's a good idea to do this?" he asked. "We might get into trouble."

"We need to save Screenfield from Crinkle-Tube by finding those books!" declared a heroic Lyla before she took a huge gulp of soy milk. "Aren't you tired of being bored?" she asked, wiping her milk mustache away with the back of her hand.

Everyone nodded in agreement.

"Aren't you tired of learning from a tube-vision?" asked Lyla.

They looked at each other and then nodded their heads up and down again. With her mouth full of cookies, Samantha replied, "You"—*crunch*—"are"—*crunch*—"correct"—*crunch*!

She stood up next to Lyla and raised her fist in the air to indicate she's on board.

"I have to be right because there is no other choice," Lyla said with a bang of her fist on the table, which caused everyone's milk glasses to wobble.

"How do we know what we are searching for?" Megan asked. "What do books even look like?"

Lyla retrieved a sharpened pencil from her pocket, along with a small, white, folded piece of paper. She unfolded the paper, placed it on the table and began to draw. When she was done, she said, "This is what a book looks like."

"What is that?" asked Nick, squinting his eyes. "That's the craziest-looking picture I've ever seen!"

Lyla looked down at her picture. Not only had she attempted to draw the book, but she had also tried to sketch her grandmother, the rocking chair, and her mom as a baby.

"Lyla," Nick said with a giggle, "it looks like something your baby brother scribbled. You draw just as bad as you write!"

"Yeah, Lyla. I don't think you drew a good picture," Samantha said, agreeing with Nick.

Megan also joined in. "It's nothing but squiggly lines."

"OK, OK, OK," sighed Lyla, stopping the flow of harsh criticism. *It may be better to just sneak into my mom's room and get the picture she showed me,* Lyla thought. *She will never know.*

"So, how are we going to know what a book looks like?" Megan asked again.

"Don't worry. I'll make sure we get a better picture," said Lyla. She stood and took a map of Screenfield out of her pocket, unfolded it, and posted it on the wall. "Like I said before, my mom told me the books were buried east of downtown Screenfield. As you guys can see, the only thing east is Program Park, and I don't think the books are buried there."

Samantha got up and took a closer look at the map. She pointed to a small dot. "No ... you're wrong!" she said. "There's a dumpsite east of Program Park."

"There is?" asked Nick, surprised.

"Yeah, Mayor Crinkle put a Do Not Enter sign there," replied Samantha.

"What's in the dumpsite?" Megan asked.

"That's where they dump all of Screenfield's garbage and chemicals from the Anything Grows Laboratory," answered Samantha. "They do experiments on stuff to see if it can grow ... like plants."

"Well, that dumpsite is where the books must be buried," said Lyla, growing more excited about the idea of finding the books.

Nick was skeptical. "That could be dangerous. I don't think we should be going there. Number one," he stated, gesturing with his fingers, "we don't have permission. And number two, we could get hurt."

"Nick, are you about to let a bunch of girls be braver than you?" Lyla asked.

He paused, looked at the Troops, pointed to himself and said, "Who? Me? I'm the bravest boy in Screenfield!" Then he stuck his chest out to show his courage. "Count me in!"

Everyone chuckled at Nick's newly found fearlessness.

Lyla took her pencil and drew a medium-sized *X* on the area representing the dumpsite. "Guys, *X* marks the spot for our book hunt," she said. "Now ... everyone go home, get your shovels, and meet me at Program Park in two hours."

"Deal!" the Troops yelled unanimously.

5

The Mysterious Seed

While Mrs. Lyte was in the kitchen feeding Joey, Lyla snuck into her parents' bedroom to get the picture. She found it in her mom's top dresser drawer beneath her socks. Lyla carefully placed the picture in her pocket, and then crept back downstairs, heading straight for the garage.

"Mom, I'm going to hang out with the Troops," Lyla yelled over her shoulder.

"Make sure you carry your jacket," her mom ordered. "It's a little nippy outside."

"I have it," Lyla responded while hitching her red, metal wagon to her orange and blue bike. She threw her denim jacket, along with her dad's shovel, in the wagon and peddled off.

Lyla arrived at Program Park at exactly three o'clock. The Troops were already there, eager to begin the book hunt. They were so excited to see Lyla.

"Did you bring a better picture of the book?" asked Nick, wiping down his bike with the rag he always carried in his back pocket.

Lyla dismounted her bike and said, "I have it." She took the picture out of her pocket and passed it around so everyone could see. "Isn't it beautiful?" she asked, watching their responses to the photograph of the book.

"It sure is amazing!" exclaimed Megan.

"How cool!" added Samantha.

"Now that we know how a book looks ... Let's get started," said Nick, impatiently handing the picture back to Lyla.

"On your bikes, Troops," she commanded loudly.

Everyone tossed their shovels in Lyla's wagon and mounted their bikes. They rode five miles east of Program Park until they saw piles of stacked garbage and a gigantic Do Not Enter sign attached to a metal gate.

"I see it," shouted Samantha, pointing with one hand and steering her bike with the other. "It's just ahead."

"Yeah ... that's the target site, Troops!" Lyla said with a grin plastered on her face.

Once they reached the dumpsite, the Troops rode a few feet and then Lyla hit her brakes. "STOP!" she shouted. "This is the spot where we'll dig."

They dismounted their bikes and pushed their kickstands down with their feet.

Nick was grossed out. "Ewww ... This place stinks!" he cried out as he pinched his nose, which made his voice sound weird.

"Why this spot?" asked Samantha. "This place is huge. Mayor Crinkle could have buried the books anywhere."

"Look around," Lyla instructed. "This is the only spot not covered by garbage," she said, her eyes sweeping over the dumpsite. "And over there are barrels of icky, green stuff spilling all over the ground."

"She's right," agreed Megan. "All over there is that green, slimy stuff. Just make sure you guys don't step in it."

Nick lifted his foot to check the bottom of his high-top sneaker. "Still clean!"

"Those belong to Anything Grows Laboratory," said Lyla, pointing to the barrels.

"You're right. It's written all over the barrels," added Megan.

"Everybody grab your shovels," Lyla commanded. "Let's get to digging."

The four of them picked up their shovels and began to dig into the soft earth. After an hour of sweating and digging, they saw no sign of the books.

Nick was the first to give up. He threw down his shovel, walked over to his bike, and pulled out his rag to start cleaning the handlebars. Even though he hated Mayor Crinkle's Good Morning song, he hummed it anyway. It was the only song he knew. But, it distracted Lyla and the other Troops.

"Nick, would you please stop humming that awful song?" Lyla asked, irritated that she and the other Troops couldn't dig in peace.

"Fine, but this is a waste of time," Nick declared. "Maybe your mom told you a BIG lie!"

"Yeah, Lyla," Megan said, agreeing with Nick as usual. She had stopped digging as well. "There's nothing out here except garbage and barrels of nasty goop everywhere."

Lyla was determined to find the books, but she knew she needed the Troops to help her out.

"The books have to be buried out here somewhere, guys. We just have to keep digging," she said, trying to get the Troops back on track.

"Well ... I'm hungry and I'm going home," declared Nick, thinking about his mom's homemade chili.

Just then there was a loud sound. *Growlll!*

"What is that?" asked Lyla, covering her ears, waiting for the sound to stop.

"Oh ... that sound was my tummy," answered Nick. "Told you I was hungry. That's why I'm going home. Who's going with me?"

Megan raised her hand and yelled, "Me!"

"Let's get out of this dump," Nick said, happy that he could recruit one of the Troops to his side.

Nick and Megan retrieved their shovels and mounted their bikes, but before they could pedal off, Samantha ran and stood in front of them with her arms wide as if she were an airplane.

"No, guys! Don't leave," she pleaded. "There must be books out here somewhere. Aren't you tired of watching CrinkleTube?"

"Digging for nothing is not any more fun,"

Nick said with one foot on his peddle and the other foot on the ground. "Let's go, Megan!"

"I'm sorry, guys," said Megan, looking at Lyla and Samantha as if she had betrayed the girls. "There's nothing out here."

They rode about thirty feet before Megan crashed into something protruding out of the ground. *BOOM!* She instantly went flying through the air, landing facedown on the ground. She looked like she was kissing the dirt.

Lyla and Samantha dashed toward the accident.

"Are you OK?" Lyla asked as she helped her friend stand up.

"I think I am," Megan replied as she brushed dirt from the patched knees of her blue jeans.

"What did you hit?" asked Nick, running over to the object sticking halfway out of the ground. He squatted to get a better look. "It's all covered with dirt."

"Maybe it's the books," said Lyla as she walked over to the object.

"I don't think it's a book because it's round

with green and white spots," observed Nick.

Lyla ran over to where she and Samantha had left their shovels, retrieved them, ran back, and then said, "Let's get it out of the ground!"

All four of the Troops grabbed their shovels and started to dig around the object. After what seemed like hours of shoveling, Lyla shouted, "Let's get it out!"

They threw their tools on the ground, grabbed its sides, and hoisted it out of the ground. The *thing* had a peculiar oval shape. It was pointy at both ends and had a smooth surface like an emerald. It was pale brown with tiny white and green spots all over it. It was the most **Mysterious Seed** they had ever seen.

"It looks like a gigantic watermelon!" said Samantha.

"It's a GIGANTIC SEED," Lyla said in surprise.

"What's a huge seed doing out here in this dumpsite?" asked Megan.

"Not growing," Nick answered sarcastically.

"We can see that," Samantha responded.

Lyla gently kicked the seed with the tip of her sneaker. "What should we do with it?"

Samantha looked at Lyla's wagon. "You should take it home for your science project and plant it to see what ger-mi-nates," she said, trying out the new vocabulary word from science class.

"I want books, not a strange-looking seed!" Lyla said angrily. "Please ... Can we dig just a little longer?"

"I sort of agree with Nick and Megan now," Samantha said. "I'm tired of digging. Let's just go home with what we found. We can always come back."

Lyla looked at the Troops' faces and admitted to herself that she was tired too. "OK," she sighed. "Let's go."

"Great!" Nick said with a huge smile. "I'm glad you're ready to join us."

If Lyla was going to take the mysterious seed home, she needed to leave right away. She knew her parents were at the grocery store, which would give her just enough time to get home with the seed before they did. If they saw it, they would ask all types of questions. And once she told them she'd been at the dumpsite, she would definitely be in trouble. Lyla looked at the purple watch on her wrist before saying, "Troops, help me put the seed in my wagon."

"OK!" they replied. Nick and Megan grabbed the shovels while Lyla and Samantha sprinted to retrieve their bikes. Together, the Troops loaded the mysterious seed into Lyla's wagon. Then they hopped on their bikes and rode off in the direction of Lyla's house.

Lyla spotted Mrs. Wilma Holmes' little, yellow Volkswagen Beetle as the Troops approached the corner of Crinkle Street and Channel Boulevard.

Mayor Crinkle had four employees working for him. Lyla's dad was the camera operator. Mr. Bruce Butler was Mayor Crinkle's driver. Ms. Julie Weatherspoon was his secretary, and Mrs. Wilma Holmes was Mayor Crinkle's neighborhood owl. She kept her big eyes wide open and was always in everyone's business. Her reports kept Mayor Crinkle in the loop with what was going on in Screenfield.

Mrs. Holmes was the tallest woman in Screenfield. Her dark black hair, which was almost as long as she was tall, flowed down her back, and she wore a size fifteen shoe (the biggest feet in Screenfield!).

Lyla knew Mrs. Holmes had seen them when she saw her struggling to get out of her car (because of her height). "Quick, throw my jacket over the seed!" Lyla ordered.

"What did you say?" Nick asked. "I didn't hear you."

"I said throw my jacket over the seed!" Lyla repeated, turning her head and projecting her voice so Nick could hear.

"Why?" Nick always wanted to know why he was asked to do something before he actually did it.

Lyla slowed down and pointed toward the corner. "Cause, there's Mrs. Holmes!"

Nick quickly jumped off his bike, grabbed Lyla's jacket out of the wagon, and tossed it over the strange seed. He turned to hop back on his bike only to bump right into Mrs. Holmes' hip.

"Hello, you Little People," she said. That was her special nickname for the Troops.

"Hi, Mrs. Holmes," they replied in unison, dismounting their bikes.

"Why do you have shovels?" she asked

suspiciously.

Lyla's jacket was not large enough to conceal all four of the shovels, so they stuck out like a sore thumb.

"For the dump—" Nick blurted without thinking. He did that all the time, especially when he was nervous and couldn't think of what to say.

Oh no! Mrs. Holmes is going to know that we went to the dumpsite, Lyla thought to herself. She had to think fast, so she interrupted Nick and said, "He means people are dumping garbage in

the neighborhood, and we are picking it up with our shovels."

Mrs. Holmes continued her interrogation. "And what's that mountain-looking object in your wagon?"

"Smelly garbage," Lyla responded, pinching her nose like an odor was coming from the wagon. "Our Tube Teacher, Mayor Crinkle, taught us to value a clean world," she added.

"How despicable the people of this town are to fling their garbage everywhere," Mrs. Holmes said angrily.

"Uh-huh," agreed the Troops, even though they had no idea what despicable meant ... and they sure weren't going to ask the definition.

Mrs. Holmes continued, "Mayor Crinkle should give a hefty fine for people who litter in Screenfield." Her attention was now diverted from what was in the wagon.

The Troops nodded in unison again. "Uh-huh."

"Great job, Little People. I'll be sure to tell Mayor Crinkle about your wonderful efforts in keeping Screenfield clean," she praised.

"Thank you," they replied.

"Until I see you again," said Mrs. Holmes, pointing with two fingers, first to her eyes, then to the Troops, and then making a peace sign, "keep up the great work. Bye-bye."

Everyone watched as Mrs. Holmes squeezed into her little Volkswagen Bug, and they all breathed a sigh of relief when she drove off.

"Lyla, now that was some fast thinking," said Megan.

"Thanks," replied Lyla. "I don't know what we would have done if Mrs. Holmes knew we were coming from the dumpsite."

"Yeah, thanks to Nick we almost got caught," said Samantha.

"I was nervous," responded Nick.

"Well, when you're nervous," continued Samantha. "You should put your hand over your mouth and don't say a word."

"Nick, tell Samantha to leave you alone," said Megan.

Before Nick could respond, Lyla interrupted, "We have no time to start pointing the finger. We have to get this seed home and bury it before my parents get home."

Everyone agreed and they rode off.

6

Overnight

"**L**et's pull the wagon to the backyard," instructed Lyla. She had lucked out! Her mom, dad, and Joey, of course, had not made it home from the store. "They should be here soon, so we have to work very fast."

"Where are you going to plant this huge seed?" asked Samantha.

"Close to my tree house," Lyla responded as she unhitched the wagon from her bike.

Lyla and Nick grasped the long, white handle of the wagon and pulled while Samantha and Megan pushed from the back. After hauling the heavy seed halfway across the well-manicured lawn, the wagon came to a halt.

"That thing is heavy!" declared Nick, huffing and puffing as if he had ran a grueling race.

"This looks like a good digging spot," Lyla said, pointing to a spot about seven feet away from her tree house. "Let's get this seed out of the wagon and into the ground quickly!"

"I agree, because I'm starving," said Nick, rubbing his growling tummy.

The Troops removed Lyla's jacket and the shovels from the wagon. Then they tilted it from the front, causing the seed to roll out with a loud thump. It hit the ground, rolled about a foot and a half, and then wobbled and stopped. They immediately began digging as fast as they could. When they were done, the hole was big enough for a fifty-inch tubevision to fit comfortably. All four hoisted the gigantic seed and lowered it gently into the hole. They poured the soil they had just dug up over the seed, recycling rather than wasting the resource. Once it was completely covered, all they saw was brown dirt and tiny pebbles.

"Now, all we need to do is water it," Lyla advised.

"Since it's so big, it might need a hundred gallons of water," said Samantha. She was the mathematical brain of their crew, so she tried to calculate how much water it would need, but she was way off.

Lyla ran to turn on the outdoor faucet and then picked up the green, snake-like water hose. She walked back to the place where they buried the seed and soaked the area and surrounding grass until it looked like a small, man-made pond. Everybody's sneakers were drenched with water.

"Lyla, I think you watered it too much," said Megan.

"I hope not," responded Lyla, sprinting away to turn off the gushing water. "Well, Troops," she said, jogging back from turning off the faucet, "I think our job is all done for the day."

Just then, the Troops heard the roaring sound of Lyla's mom and dad's van pulling into the driveway.

"Here come your parents!" said Samantha, her eyes bulging at the thought of Mr. and Mrs. Lyte catching them with wet sneakers in the backyard. Everyone turned their heads to look in Samantha's direction.

Nick saw the van too, and even though he knew the seed was resting in the ground, he still got nervous. "I'm out!" he said as he trotted to his bike.

"I'm out too!" added Megan, trailing behind Nick as usual.

"Me too!" cosigned Samantha.

Lyla's dad stepped out of the van carrying several bags of groceries, while her mom opened the back door to take Joey out of the car seat.

"Hi, bye, Mr. and Mrs. Lyte," everyone said with a wave before jumping on their bikes and peddling off. The Troops left Lyla by herself. No one waved good-bye to her.

The next morning, while Lyla and Joey sat around the oval kitchen table eating their Sunday breakfast (Joey was actually playing with his scrambled eggs ... not eating them), Lyla's mom was preparing to work in her garden. She put on her garden pants decorated with a community of printed tulips and her white, short-sleeve shirt with a big, round, yellow happy face on the front. She also wore her yellow garden gloves and her wide straw hat to block bright sunrays.

"Lyla, make sure Joey eats all of his breakfast," she instructed before walking out the back door.

"Ahhh man ... He doesn't listen to me," Lyla said with a smirk on her face.

Before she could turn her head, Joey flung a scrambled egg that smacked Lyla in the center of her forehead.

"Gaht you!" he said, giggling like a hyena.

"Mommm!" Lyla yelled, ready to pounce on Joey like a tiger.

Mrs. Lyte came rushing back inside the house.

Lyla thought she was coming to her rescue, but she was totally wrong.

"Lyla, do you know about that odd plant growing next to your tree house?" she asked hysterically.

Lyla immediately forgot all about the flying scrambled eggs. "It already grew?" she said before she dropped her fork and darted to the back door.

"Where do you think you're go—" Lyla's mom started to ask as her daughter nearly knocked her down to get outside.

"Wow! It grew **Overnight**!" Lyla said in utter amazement as she stared at the towering plant.

She looked up at the sprouting green stem with its leaves shooting out at the top. Lyla touched the thick stem, and to her surprise, it was as hard as a wooden door. "That's strange!"

"Lyla, get yourself in this house!" Mrs. Lyte called loudly. "You still have your pajamas on. Don't you know we have nosy neighbors?"

Lyla glanced down at her pink pajamas and matching socks, and then back up at the plant.

Not wanting to take her eyes off the peculiar plant, she walked backward to the house, getting grass and dirt stains on the bottom of her socks along the way.

"Take off those filthy socks before you gallop through this house, young lady," ordered Mrs. Lyte. "I don't want grass, dirt, and insect POOH-POOH on my clean carpet!"

"Mom, insects don't use the bathroom," Lyla

disputed as she leaned on the door frame to remove her socks.

"Yes, they do ... in our backyard. You just don't see them pooh-poohing," responded Mrs. Lyte.

Lyla looked disgusted. "Ewww ... that's nasty!" she said. She dropped her socks on the floor and headed to the bathroom to scrub her hands with soap and warm water.

Satisfied that she had removed all traces of possible insect pooh-pooh from her hands, Lyla turned the water off. She was about to reach for the tulip hand towels that hung neatly on the towel rack when she heard her mother ask, "How did that plant find a home in my backyard?"

"It's my science project," Lyla answered as tiny droplets of water dripped from her fingertips.

"Well, I hope your science project doesn't experiment on my tulips," Lyla's mom said as she opened and closed her pruning shears like she was cutting weeds in her garden. "Because you know what I do to pesky weeds."

"It's a plant, Mom, not a weed," Lyla responded.

Mrs. Lyte refused to go back and forth with her daughter on the topic of whether or not the huge *thing* in her backyard was a plant or a weed. "So, what are you supposed to do with that odd-looking plant?" she asked.

"Just watch it grow," Lyla answered.

"Do you have to write anything for school?" her mom asked.

"No!" Lyla replied promptly. "If I had to, I would get another *F* anyway since I'm terrible at writing."

Mrs. Lyte paused a moment, put her pruning shears down outside the back door, took off her gloves and said, "Lyla … don't you worry. One day you will be able to use your imagination and write beautiful essays."

"When will that day be?" Lyla asked, doubting her mother's words. She tilted her head down toward the floor and studied her hands.

"Just be patient, dear. That day will come," Mrs. Lyte said as she placed a finger beneath Lyla's chin and pushed it up until their eyes met.

"I believe you will be one of the best writers in the whole entire world."

"Do you really believe that?" Lyla asked as she began to crack a smile.

Lyla's mom looked deep into her eyes and said, "Yes ... I do."

For those feel-good words, Lyla gave her mom the tightest hug, coupled with a double dose of "I love you, I love you!"

"OK, OK ... my hips can't breathe," Mrs. Lyte said with a giggle a few seconds later.

"Now, can I go back outside?" Lyla asked, anxiously waiting for the answer.

"Yes," replied her mom. Then she began waving her finger in the air. "But you have to do one thing first."

Lyla sighed. "What's that?"

"Go change your clothes," her mother ordered.

"That's it?" Lyla said. "I thought you were going to say something like *go clean up your bedroom!*"

They both laughed because they knew that would have taken Lyla all day to finish.

7

First Taste of Imagination

Monday morning finally came. Lyla woke up at 6:45 a.m. without her parents having to wake her up. She was extremely excited to see how much the plant had grown overnight. She flung her orange comforter onto the carpeted floor of her bedroom and raced to the window to look out at the backyard. What she saw left her stunned. The plant had grown into a towering, and very leafy, tree that soared up past her tree house.

"Wow!" shouted Lyla. She squinted and rubbed her eyes. "I can't believe what I'm seeing! And fruit grew on it too!" Lyla said in amazement. "But they look so ... strange."

She moved nearer to the window to get a better look at the bizarre fruit hanging from the branches.

"I still can't tell what type of fruit that is," she said aloud. "I just have to go outside to get a closer look!"

Lyla dashed to the bathroom, brushed her teeth, and washed her face. Then, she returned to her bedroom where she quickly threw on her school clothes before heading down the hallway.

"Lyla, why are you up so early?" her dad asked before she could make it to the stairs. He had opened his door because he thought he heard someone moving about. He was stunned to see Lyla up before he or his wife could wake her. "You're already dressed?" he asked in amazement.

Lyla stopped at the top of the stairs. "I'm going to check on my science project."

"I've never seen you get so thrilled over schoolwork before," Mr. Lyte responded.

"Well, this is a special project," Lyla said enthusiastically.

"OK," her dad said before retreating into his bedroom to get dressed.

Once downstairs, Lyla was so excited to see the tree close up that she fumbled with the lock on

the back door. When she finally got it open, her eyes nearly bulged out of her head at the sight of the tree.

"This is amazing!" Lyla said as she gazed upward.

She walked over to the massive trunk to get a closer look at the fruit hanging from the limbs.

"That's not fruit!" Lyla exclaimed in astonishment. "Those are BOOKS!"

And the tree was filled with small books, big books, and different colored books. There were paperback books and hardback books. There were pictures of people, animals, objects, and places on the covers, accompanied by short names and long names of titles, authors, and illustrators. They all dangled from the branches surrounded by rich green leaves.

Lyla stood on her tippy-toes to grab one, but it was too high to reach. She jumped to get a book, but still she was unsuccessful. *They're too high,* she said to herself as she walked around the tree looking at all the books. Then, she glanced over at her tree house and noticed something that made her smile even more. *Some of the tree's branches went through the window of the tree house!*

"That's it! That's it! That's how I'll be able to get a book!" Lyla shouted and jumped up and down with excitement.

She quickly climbed up the wooden planks, opened the door and was welcomed by branches filled with books. Lyla walked to the window, and without any hesitation, she plucked a book right off the tree.

"*The Princess and the Frog,*" she said, reading the title aloud. She stood there rubbing its hard cover in awe. "How did this tree grow all these books?" she wondered. "I've never seen anything like this before!"

Lyla sat down on her small, wooden chair. "She is so pretty!" Lyla said aloud as she stared at the illustration of Princess Tiana on the front cover.

"But why is the frog trying to kiss her?" she asked herself. "I guess the only way to find out is to read." She opened the book and instantly found herself immersed in reading. Her eyes were as bright as the morning sun, and a huge grin sprawled across her face as she flipped each page.

She was overwhelmed by the colorful pictures, and her brain was like a sponge absorbing new words and phrases like *magic, beautiful princess, gumbo, jazz, masquerade ball, flickering, fairy tales, heartbroken, pretty as a magnolia, sweetest firefly in all creation, wicked shadow, sinister man* (she thought of Mayor Crinkle), *romantic, smooch,* and *dazzling evening star.*

Lyla's **First Taste of Imagination** was love at first read. Before she knew it, she was at the end of the book. She turned the last page, closed the book, and hugged it tightly to her chest.

She never would have guessed that she could be filled with this much excitement from reading.

"Books are the most magical, dazzling, and

beautiful thing in all creation!" she declared, using her newfound vocabulary. "Finding that seed was the best thing that ever happened to me!"

She was about to pluck another book from the branch when she heard her mother call out, "Lyla, come set the table and eat!"

My mom must not have seen the tree. I have to tell my parents. If someone sees these books, they are going to tell the sinister Mayor Crinkle, Lyla thought, starting to panic. *And my dad will lose his job, and the family will end up in jail.*

"LYLA!" her mom called again.

Lyla descended the tree house stairs and walked slowly into the kitchen with a book behind her back. "Mom, I have something to show you," Lyla said hesitantly.

"Did that ugly plant sprout into a lovely tulip?" Mrs. Lyte asked.

"No ... It grew this!" Lyla said as she pulled the book from behind her back to show her mother.

At the sight of the book, Mrs. Lyte dropped the pot of half-cooked scrambled eggs on the kitchen floor. "Where did you get that?" she asked.

"It came off the tree in the backyard," Lyla responded.

"Young lady, that's impossible. Now tell me the truth!" Mrs. Lyte demanded.

"Let me show you," Lyla said.

She grabbed her mother's arm and led her through the back door. They left the runny eggs splattered all over the floor. When they walked into the backyard, her mom stood in shock before the tall tree.

"Where did this tree come from?" she asked.

"This is the plant you saw yesterday," Lyla explained. "Samantha, Megan, Nick, and I found the seed at the dumpsite."

"What were you guys doing in the dumpsite?" Mrs. Lyte asked as she turned her gaze from the tree to her daughter.

"We were ... looking for books," Lyla answered hesitantly.

"Who gave you the idea to look for books in a dumpsite?" her mom asked angrily.

Lyla pointed to her mom and said, "You did!"

"Me?" asked Lyla's mom, surprised.

She swiftly grabbed Lyla by the arm, pulled her back into the house, and slammed the door shut. "Young lady ... I specifically told you to keep the story about the books a secret!"

Lyla looked at her mom innocently before saying, "You told me not to tell *anyone*. I only told my best friends!"

"I meant everyone!" Mrs. Lyte said angrily. "And that included all of your little friends! Well, now you have to tell one more person."

"Who?" Lyla asked in a panic because she knew who her mom was talking about.

"Your dad!" her mom yelled.

Oh no! Lyla thought as her heart plunged into her tummy. *I don't want to tell him!* She concealed the book behind her back again, afraid of what her father would say when he saw it.

"HONEY!" Mrs. Lyte called.

Lyla's dad came rushing into the room. "What is it?" he asked.

Mrs. Lyte pushed Lyla in front of her. "Your daughter has something to show you," she said, crossing her arms and waiting for Lyla to tell her dad about the plant ... and the books. "Go ahead, young lady," she demanded, placing her hands on her hips.

Lyla closed her eyes and slowly pulled the book from behind her back. As soon her dad saw the book, he dropped to the floor like a sack of Russet potatoes and passed out.

Mrs. Lyte splashed cold water on her husband's face. He came to, blinked his eyes rapidly, and asked, "Where did that book come from?"

"I'll show you," Lyla said, helping her dad up off the floor.

She took his hand and led him to the backyard. Mrs. Lyte decided to stay behind to clean up the eggs before they got all hard and crusty and permanently stained the kitchen tile.

In the backyard, Lyla and her father stood in front of the massive tree.

"This is unbelievable! This is impossible!" he said in amazement.

"I know," Lyla responded.

He turned his head and looked at his daughter. "Lyla, how did this happen! And why is this tree in my backyard?"

"Well ..." she began hesitantly, "you know Samantha ... and Megan ... and Nick ... and ... well ... We went to the dumpsite ... and we found this seed ... and—"

"STOP!" her dad yelled. "I don't want to hear any more."

"But!"

"That's enough."

"I just—"

"I said I don't want to hear any more," Mr. Lyte commanded. "I can't believe there's a tree in my backyard that has sprouted books."

Lyla didn't let another word fly from her mouth.

Suddenly, her dad dashed frantically toward the garage. Lyla ran behind him to see what he was going to do.

"We have to get those books off that tree before our neighbors start leaving for work," he said.

Mr. Lyte opened the garage door and grabbed his four-foot ladder. "Go get the large laundry basket and the broom," he ordered.

Lyla ran to the laundry room, retrieved the basket, and snatched the broom from her mom, who was busy cleaning up scrambled eggs. "Dad needs it," she said and ran out the door.

"Hand me the broom," Mr. Lyte instructed. "And put the basket next to Mom's tulips."

One by one, he knocked the books off the

branches with the broomstick. They fell like apples from an apple tree. When the basket was full, Mr. Lyte grabbed it and climbed up the ladder into the tree house. Once inside, he dumped the books on the floor. They repeated this process for what seemed like hours until the tree limbs were bare and the two of them were exhausted.

As soon as they sat down to rest, they heard Mrs. Lyte call from the back door. "There's no time to rest, you two. You are going to be late for work and school!"

"Oh no!" Mr. Lyte yelled as he ran inside and up the stairs to get his tie and suit jacket.

"Lyla," Mrs. Lyte began as she wiped the sweat off of her daughter's face, "I want you to ask Samantha, Megan, and Nick to come over here after school. We have to make sure they keep this a secret."

"I will," Lyla said gladly.

8

The Secret Name

L yla arrived late to school, and she couldn't wait to tell the Troops about the books. When she entered Room 201, the tubevision screen was blank, which was weird because it was always on at that time.

"We will be starting school late this morning," Ms. Verdak announced from the front of the class. She stopped speaking abruptly when she noticed Lyla tiptoeing toward her seat. "Nice of you to join us," she said.

Lyla couldn't offer anything but an apology. "Sorry, Ms. Verdak."

"If you were sorry, you would start being on time for school," Mary Englemouth said sarcastically.

"Why don't you mind your own business," Lyla retorted.

"Lyla and Mary, that's enough!" Ms. Verdak said sternly, interrupting their soon-to-be argument. "Everyone, we will go outside early today."

Room 201 became excited and chanted, "No CrinkleTube! No CrinkleTube!"

"That's enough!" Ms. Verdak told the class with a scowl on her face. "Everyone, line up."

This timing is perfect! Lyla thought. Now she wouldn't have to wait until after lunch to tell the Troops. She could let them in on the big secret now.

Everyone lined up and headed through the double doors.

Lyla was very anxious as the Troops gathered under the monkey bars. "You guys will never guess what happened to the seed," she said with a smile.

"It grew tulips?" Samantha guessed.

"No!" Lyla promptly responded. "That's the same thing my mom said. Come on, try again."

"You got into trouble for planting it," Nick answered, taking his turn at guessing what happened to the seed.

Lyla squeezed her slender fingers together as if she were holding a bean. "A little. But that happened after the big surprise."

"Tell us already," Megan ordered. She was tired of the guessing game and wanted to know what the big surprise was.

"OK," Lyla said before pausing to look at each of their faces. "It grew books!"

"BOOKS!" bellowed Nick.

Lyla immediately placed her hand over Nick's mouth to shut him up. Nick repeated the word with a muffled voice.

"You want the whole world to know?" Lyla exclaimed.

Nick shook his head back and forth and then looked around to make sure no one heard what he said.

"Did I hear you correctly?" asked Samantha. "That strange-looking seed grew books?

"Yeah," Lyla answered, her hand still covering Nick's mouth.

"OK … you can remove your hand now," Nick mumbled through Lyla's fingers.

She removed her hand and smelled it. "Ewww!" she said.

"How did the seed do that?" Megan asked.

Lyla shrugged. "I don't know. I woke up this morning and there it was—a huge tree filled with all kinds of books."

"Can we see the tree after school?" asked Nick.

"Of course," Lyla replied. "Besides, my mom wants everybody to come over after school anyway."

"Mom!" Lyla yelled as she and the Troops entered the house. They knew they were in store for something important because they weren't welcomed by the smell of fresh-baked cookies.

Lyla's mom came down the stairs holding Joey. "Hello, children," she said, greeting the Troops.

"Hi, Mrs. Lyte," they all said.

"Everyone, please sit down," Mrs. Lyte instructed.

"No cookies *and* we have to sit," Nick whispered to Samantha. "We must be in a lot of trouble."

"I don't know for what," Samantha whispered back.

Once everyone was seated, Mrs. Lyte asked,

"Did Lyla tell all of you about the books?"

Everyone nodded, even Lyla. "Yeah."

"We don't know how this happened," Mrs. Lyte said sternly, "but we must keep this a secret. If Mayor Crinkle finds out, all of us are going to end up in jail."

"JAIL? I don't want to go to jail ... I don't want to go to jail!" Nick cried hysterically. "I'm too young!"

Lyla slapped Nick lightly across his right cheek.

"Ouch!" yelled Nick. "What did you do that for?"

"You need to get yourself together," Lyla said, looking at him with a serious expression on her face. "Wipe those tears. None of us are going to jail."

"Lyla is right," said her mom, "as long as we keep the books a secret."

"Don't worry, Mrs. Lyte," Samantha said. "We will keep them a secret."

Everyone nodded in agreement, except Megan ... but no one noticed.

"Great!" Mrs. Lyte said. "Lyla, you can take

them out back to see the books now."

The Troops jumped up and rushed to the door, nearly knocking each other down on the way.

"What a huge tree!" Samantha exclaimed once they stepped into the backyard.

"It's hard to believe that this gigantic tree grew from the seed we found," said Megan as she touched the tree trunk.

Nick walked around the tree looking upward. "But ... where are the books?" he asked.

"They are in the tree house," answered Lyla. "My dad and I knocked them off the tree this morning so our neighbors wouldn't see them."

"What are we standing outside for then? To the tree house!" Nick shouted excitedly.

One by one, they climbed into the tree house.

Everyone was in awe of what they saw inside.

"Un—real!"

"Incredible!"

"I can't believe my eyes!"

Lyla stood watching the Troops react to the books with a big grin on her face.

"Isn't—it—dazzling!" she said with a twinkle in her eye.

All of the Troops nodded and then turned back to the books, which were scattered all over the floor.

Nick picked up a paperback. "*Superman!*" he said, reading the title aloud.

Then, he began asking a basketful of questions. "Why is he showing his red underwear? Why does he have a red sheet on his back?"

"Read it and find out," Lyla suggested excitedly.

Nick took Lyla's advice. He sat on a chair, quickly opened the book, and dived right in.

Megan leaned her chair against the wall and held on to the back of it with her left hand. In her other hand, she held tight to her book. Then, she lifted her right leg in the air behind her and began to wobble.

"I can't keep my balance!" she exclaimed.

"Don't fall!" Lyla warned. But it was too late.

CRASH! Megan fell and landed on a pile of books.

"What were you trying do?" Lyla asked as she helped Megan up off the books.

"Ballet," Megan answered exuberantly. "I'm reading *How to be Brilliant at Ballet.*"

"Well ... you keep on reading and practicing," Lyla instructed as if she were a reading coach.

"Two mul-ti-plied by three equals six. I GOT IT! I GOT IT!" Samantha yelled after checking the back of the workbook to make sure the answer to her math question was correct. "This is the greatest book ever."

"What's the name of it?" Lyla asked.

"*Multiplication Facts Made Easy*," Samantha said, reading the title aloud. "We never learn this type of math at Crinkle Academy."

As Lyla stepped over books to avoid trampling them, one caught her attention. She picked it up and mumbled, "*Karate Katie*." Lyla turned the book over and read the summary to herself.

"Lyla, what's that book about?" Samantha asked as she walked over to her.

"The back says it's about someone who can break wood and fly around in the air," Lyla answered. Then she flipped the book over to look at the cover again. "It must be her—Katie."

"That sounds so cool," Samantha said while looking at the picture of Karate Katie over Lyla's shoulder.

Lyla was ecstatic. Not only did she enjoy reading, but her friends did too. "Troops, sorry to disturb your reading time, but I need you all over here."

The group of friends stopped reading their

books and made their way to the side of the tree house where Lyla was standing. Once the Troops were seated around the little table with their books clasped in their hands, Lyla said, "We need a way to keep the books a secret from Mayor Crinkle."

"That's going to be hard to do," Nick declared. "Maybe we should just *not read them!*"

"*I would rather kiss a hundred frogs,*" exclaimed Lyla, perking her lips.

"You would do what?" the Troops asked in unison and looked at Lyla baffled.

"I got that from a book I read called *The Princess and the Frog,*" Lyla explained.

Suddenly, Nick shouted excitedly, "It's in my book! It's in my book!"

"What's in your book?" Lyla asked.

"It tells us how we can keep the books a secret," answered Nick.

"What does it say?" the girls asked, confused, and growing a little impatient with Nick.

Nick quickly flipped his book open. "In here, Superman has a secret name."

"First, who is Superman?" asked Megan.

112

Nick showed them the colorful illustrations. "He has superpowers."

"What type of superpowers?" asked Lyla.

"He can lift cars, fly in the sky, and he is faster than a speeding bullet," explained Nick. "He also saves people!"

Lyla was confused. "So what does this have to do with keeping the books a secret?"

"He has a secret name so no one will know he's Superman!" Nick replied.

"What is his secret name?" asked Samantha.

"Clark Kent," answered Nick.

"Sooo ... We should call the books Clark Kent?" Megan asked with a puzzled expression.

Nick shook his head frantically. "No ... another name!"

"Ohhh ... I get it," Lyla said. "We should give the *books* a secret name."

"Finally, Nick said something that made sense," declared Samantha, patting Nick on the back. "That's a great idea!"

"What should **The Secret Name** be?" Megan asked.

"The books grew on trees like fruit," replied Lyla. "Sooo ... fruit should be part of the name."

"What type of fruit?" asked Samantha. "Bananas ... apples ... strawberries?"

Suddenly, Lyla remembered her conversation with the Troops on the playground when she told them about the books.

"Nick, say the word *library*," she instructed.

He hesitated. "Why? So you can make fun of me?" he asked.

"Just say the word!" Lyla demanded.

"OK ... li'berry." He spat it out quickly with his arms folded.

"That's it!" beamed Lyla, standing up. "We'll call books ... LI'BERRY FRUIT!"

Samantha jumped out of her chair and gave Lyla a high-five. *CLAP!*

"I like it!" Samantha said with a huge grin.

"Are you sure?" asked Megan. "Everyone is going to think we're talking about food."

"Exactly!" Lyla said. "That's perfect! Mayor Crinkle will never know that Li'berries are BOOKS!"

The Troops turned to Nick for his approval. He gave them a thumbs-up. "And most importantly," he said, "we don't have to go to jail."

"All in favor of the name Li'berry Fruit, raise your books in the air," instructed Lyla, raising her book first.

The rest of the Troops followed and began to chant, "Li'berry Fruit ... Li'berry Fruit."

"Now, remember," Lyla said, "don't tell *anyone* about Li'berry Fruit!"

9

Big Plans

Monday morning came, and Lyla woke up not believing yesterday's unbelievable events. She lay in bed thinking that it was all one big dream. *Could there finally be something other than CrinkleTube in Screenfield?* Lyla thought to herself. After daydreaming for a while, she decided to get out of bed and see if the tree was still in the backyard.

"Oh my GOSH!" Lyla exclaimed, stunned by what she saw outside her window. A bunch of books grew on the tree all over again. "Yippee, yippee!" Lyla shouted with glee.

When Lyla's dad heard her cheering, he rushed to her room and hesitantly opened the

116

door. "I don't really want to know, but from the sound of it, should I assume the books are back?"

Lyla nodded with a smile.

"This can't be happening," her father groaned as he went to pull out his hair. "Books aren't supposed to grow on trees."

"They do in Screenfield!" Lyla said while bouncing up and down on her bed. "I'll get the basket and broom, and you get the ladder," she added as she hopped off of the bed and ran to get her school clothes.

Mr. Lyte retreated to his bedroom to get dressed.

His wife asked, "What happened?"

"Those dang ol' books are back," he replied.

"It seems like that tree is going to grow new books every morning," Mrs. Lyte said from her side of the bed.

"I hope not, because I will go crazy!" Mr. Lyte said as he put his undershirt on. "I do not need this in my life. If Mayor Crinkle finds out, you know what will happen," he said, hopping around the room with one leg in his dress pants.

"Look on the bright side," Mrs. Lyte said, laughing at the sight of her husband moving about.

"I didn't know there was one," Mr. Lyte responded sarcastically.

Mrs. Lyte curled her arms to flex her muscles. "You get to exercise in the morning."

"Ha ... ha ... ha!" he chuckled. "So you're saying I'm out of shape?"

Before Mrs. Lyte had a chance to respond, Lyla yelled up the stairs, "Dad, let's get to work. The neighbors will be leaving for work really soon."

"Go ... before that child wakes Joey up," Mrs. Lyte said, flopping back on her fluffy pillows.

Lyla's dad walked down the stairs and made a beeline for the garage to get the ladder. He hoisted it onto his shoulder and carried it over to the tree, where Lyla was waiting with the laundry basket and broom.

"Oh no ... It seems like more books than

yesterday. Can it get any worse?" he grumbled, shaking his head. "This is going to take longer than I expected. This is horrible. Why me? And why my backyard!"

"Well ... let's get started," Lyla said, ignoring her dad's rambling.

The duo made more trips than they did the day before. Back and forth, they plucked books and dumped them inside the tree house. Before they knew it, piles of books were stacked from floor to ceiling.

"If that tree grows more books, we are going to have to put them inside the house," Mr. Lyte said.

That was like sweet music to Lyla's ears. "If we do, can we keep the books in my bedroom?" she asked. She looked at her dad with big puppy dog eyes before adding a please for good measure.

"Hopefully we don't have to make that decision," her dad replied. "Let's just focus on getting all of these books off the tree this morning."

When they were finally done, there were so many books in the tree house that Lyla couldn't walk inside without trampling on a book.

"I finally found true happiness," she declared as she stood in the child-size doorway of her tree house. She was as happy as a kid in a candy store.

"Lyla, let's go," her dad shouted from the base of the tree. He stood there waiting for Lyla to come down so he could put the ladder back in the garage. "We're going to be late again. Let's hurry up, eat our breakfast, and get up out of here."

"Rating, ratings, ratings!" boasted Mayor Crinkle, hugging his enormous seventy-inch tubevision in his luxurious office suite. He gave the screen a big kiss, leaving a wet imprint from his lips. "I love that my viewer ratings are up. They are higher than ever before. Everyone in Screenfield just loves watching CrinkleTube!"

The phone rang outside Mayor Crinkle's office suite. *RING ... RING ... RING.*

"City Hall ... How can I help you?" Ms. Weatherspoon answered with her friendly tone.

"I would like to talk to the mayor," the caller requested with a deep voice. "Is he available?"

"May I ask who's calling?" said Ms. Weatherspoon.

"My name is Mr. Sam P. Simpson," answered the caller.

"Please hold on. I will see if the mayor is

available." Ms. Weatherspoon placed the caller on hold and clicked over to the other line. "Mayor Crinkle, someone on the phone wants to talk to you."

Mayor Crinkle was annoyed by the interrupttion. "Who is it?" he asked harshly. He sat behind his huge, mahogany desk with gold legs. His matching leather chair was so big that it swallowed him up. "I hope this is not another needy person calling me," he muttered under his breath.

"A gentleman by the name of Mr. Sam P. Simpson," answered Ms. Weatherspoon.

"Mr. Simpson?" Mayor Crinkle said, jogging his memory to see if he had met him previously. His name didn't ring a bell. "What does this stranger want?"

"He didn't tell me, sir," Ms. Weatherspoon politely replied. "Do you want me to transfer the call?"

After a short pause, Mayor Crinkle said, "Go ahead and connect him."

When the phone rang in his office, the mayor answered, "This is your number one illustrious mayor of Screenfield. What can I do for you today?"

"I would like to obtain a permit to have my own tubevision program for children," the caller said proudly. "I have a great idea that they will truly love."

Mayor Crinkle became irritated. "What do mean your own show? Who is this?" he demanded, clutching the phone tighter.

"My name is Mr. Sam P. Simpson," responded the caller. "I plan on producing my own show."

"I'll not approve that request," Mayor Crinkle yelled into the phone.

The caller was confused. "But I haven't submitted my application yet," he responded. "Isn't there a process I have to go through?"

"You don't need to submit anything. I'm telling you your request is denied!" Mayor Crinkle said firmly. "I will be the only one with a show in Screenfield!"

"Well, I'll just take my program to another town!" the caller yelled back. "The children are right. You are the worst mayor ever!"

"Thanks, and good riddance to you!" Mayor Crinkle said, slamming the phone down and hanging up on the caller. "The nerve of these good-for-nothing people in Screenfield!" he said angrily to himself.

Ms. Weatherspoon became concerned when she heard Mayor Crinkle screaming on the phone. She got up and knocked on his door. "Is everything OK, sir?" she asked.

"I need you in my office. NOW!" he commanded.

Ms. Weatherspoon entered cautiously. "What do you need, sir?" she asked. "Do I need to get my pen and a piece of paper?"

"No," answered Mayor Crinkle. "Just tell Mr. Lyte that I want to see him."

Ms. Weatherspoon took a quick peek in the hallway. "He called this morning to say that he would be late," she responded.

Mayor Crinkle was livid. He banged his fist on the desk and said, "I have **Big Plans** for CrinkleTube. If he wants to be a part of the future, he'd better start being on time for work."

As soon as Mayor Crinkle made that statement, there was a sudden ruckus in the hallway. Mr. Lyte had come rushing into City Hall, as if right on cue, and managed to trip over his own feet. He entered Mayor Crinkle's office huffing and puffing.

"Sorry I'm late, sir," Mr. Lyte said. "I had to drop my daughter at—"

"I don't have time for petty excuses," Mayor

Crinkle said. "Just take a seat, Mr. Lyte." Mayor Crinkle pointed to the black leather chair in front of his desk.

Then, he turned his attention to Ms. Weatherspoon. "You can go back to your desk," he said, dismissing her. "And no more phone calls for the day!"

Ms. Weatherspoon walked out of the office, closing the door behind her as she left.

"I have some bad news!" began Mayor Crinkle.

He found out about the books. I'm going to get fired ... Oh no! Mr. Lyte thought as he sat and began to bite his fingernails.

Mayor Crinkle continued, "I do not need you as the camera operator anymore."

Sweat rolled down Mr. Lyte's forehead. "Mayor Crinkle ... please ... I'm sooo sorry!"

Mayor Crinkle was puzzled. "Sorry for what?" he asked. "That I'm promoting you to a better and higher-paying position."

Now it was Mr. Lyte's turn to be confused. "Come again?"

"I'm taking CrinkleTube global!" explained the mayor. "I want my channel to be on every tubevision in the entire world, and I want you to be the new Director of Marketing to ensure that CrinkleTube becomes a worldwide name."

"Who?" Mr. Lyte asked, still a bit confused but very relieved by the news. "Me?"

"I know it's a lot to take on, Mr. Lyte, but I trust you," declared Mayor Crinkle.

"Who?" Mr. Lyte asked again. "Me?"

Mayor Crinkle became annoyed. "Mr. Lyte! Am I talking to an owl?" he asked.

He shook his head. "No, sir."

"That's good to know, because I don't need an owl. I need you to be a lion if we are going to take over the world," he said. "Now, let me here you roar!"

Mr. Lyte let out a soft sound. "Roarrr ..."

"Is that the best you can do?" the mayor asked. "Stand on the chair and act like you are king of the jungle."

Mr. Lyte stood on the chair, bared his teeth, and growled, "ROARRR!"

"That's more like it," Mayor Crinkle said with glee. "Now get down and wipe off my chair."

As Mr. Lyte jumped off the chair, he accidently knocked the mayor's white coffee cup—which had a picture of his face on it—off the edge of his desk. It hit the floor and instantly shattered to pieces.

"Mr. Lyte, I hope you don't break my trust like you just broke my special cup," said Mayor

Crinkle, peeking over his desk to look at the mess. "You are my best employee, so don't prove me wrong."

"You can count on me, sir," said Mr. Lyte, nodding his head in confirmation as he carefully picked the broken pieces up off the floor and placed them in the small, blue trash can. "I won't let you down."

"I hope not," Mayor Crinkle snarled. "Be ready next month to take over the world with CrinkleTube!"

10

Karate Lyla

When Lyla got to school, she encountered a tall, skinny girl with puffy hair. She stopped Lyla in the hallway when she was heading to class.

"Is your name Lyla Lyte?" asked the puffy-haired student.

"Yes," Lyla replied cautiously. "Why?"

"I heard you had Li'berry Fruit," she replied. "Can I have one?"

Lyla was utterly shocked. *Who could have told her about Li'berry Fruit?* Megan was the first name that popped into her head. "She can't keep a secret to herself for nothing," Lyla grumbled.

"Excuse me?" the puffy-haired student said, thinking Lyla was responding to her question.

"Oh, ummm ... nothing," Lyla replied, already thinking about what she was going to say to Megan. "I'm all out of Li'berry Fruit today," she told the girl before going to find Megan.

All of the students in Room 201 were waiting for Ms. Verdak to return from taking the attendance count to the main office. When Lyla entered, she saw Megan allowing another student to peek into her cinch sack. The second Megan's eyes caught Lyla's, she closed it up quickly.

"I'll show you later," she hastily told the student.

"Megan, what are you hiding?" asked Lyla.

"Nothing," Megan replied with a slight attitude. "There's not one thing in here."

Lyla didn't believe her. She snatched Megan's cinch sack, reached inside, and pulled out the Li'berry Fruit *How to be Brilliant at Ballet*. Lyla had caught her red-handed.

"You were reading this *fruit* yesterday!" Lyla said to Megan. "How many people did you tell?"

Lyla unconsciously waved the Li'berry Fruit in the air for everyone to see.

"LOOK! It's a Li'berry Fruit!" Johnny shouted across the room.

Suddenly, all of the students turned to see what Johnny was talking about. They got up and scrambled over to Megan and Lyla, and soon the two girls were surrounded by the entire class.

"Shhhh," Lyla said as she pressed her fingers against her lips. "We are all going to get into trouble when Ms. Verdak comes back."

No one listened. Instead, they bombarded Lyla with questions.

"How can we get a Li'berry Fruit?"

"Where did you get it?"

"Isn't that the strangest fruit you ever saw?"

"Can you eat it?"

Lyla panicked. She didn't really know what to say. All she wanted was for them to return to their seats before Ms. Verdak came back.

"OK ... Follow me to my tree house after school," she instructed as she pushed her classmates away.

Out of the blue, Mary Englemouth snatched the Li'berry Fruit out of Lyla's hand.

"Give that back to me," Lyla demanded. "It's not yours!"

"It is now!" Mary Englemouth said as she walked to the back of the room. "What are you gonna do? Write a letter to Ms. Verdak? Oh, I forgot! You got an *F* ... You CAN'T write."

I've had it, Lyla thought. She took a deep breath and removed her thin black belt from around her waist and wrapped it around her head. She untucked her shirt, allowing it to hang loose, and then slipped off her flip-flops one at a time, leaving herself barefoot.

"Instead of Karate Katie ... I'm Karate Lyla," she mumbled.

"HA, HA, HA!" Mary Englemouth jeered hysterically as she pointed at Lyla. "I've been waiting for this for a long time." Then she looked at the other students and growled, "Now get out of my way!"

Everybody, except Lyla, scrambled to the other side of the room.

Mary Englemouth tossed the Li'berry Fruit down and ran full speed toward Lyla. When she got close enough, Lyla jumped up in the air and flipped forward, causing Mary Englemouth to run straight into the tubevision cart, making the tubevision wobble before it crashed to the ground.

Lyla landed on top of another student's desk, knocking the yardstick off of Ms. Verdak's desk and into the air straight at her. She swung her arm back, stiffened her hand, yelled, *"Keeyah!"* and broke the yardstick in two.

"Wowww!" the class said in unison. All of their

mouths were open, making huge *O*s. When all the ruckus was over, the tubevision lay smashed on the classroom floor.

Lyla got down from the desk just in time before Ms. Verdak returned.

"Who broke the tubevision?" she asked angrily.

To prevent Ms. Verdak from investigating further, Lyla said, "I apologize. I was going to get the stapler off your desk and tripped over someone's cinch sack on the floor."

Ms. Verdak told Lyla and the class to be more careful and called down to the janitor to clean up the mess.

After school, Lyla's entire class followed her like a small parade to the tree house. Lyla had never had this many friends go home with her before.

Mrs. Lyte was working in her garden while Joey ran around her trying to catch a butterfly that was fluttering around the yard. He was the first to see Lyla leading the procession.

"Lyl, Lyl," Joey called out as he pointed in his sister's direction. He didn't know how to pronounce the *a* in Lyla's name yet.

When Mrs. Lyte saw the children approaching the house, she immediately threw her gardening tool to the ground and jumped up to meet the group at the gate.

"Lyla, who are all these children?" she asked, locking the gate and barricading it with her hip so no one else could enter. "And why are they all with you?"

Lyla responded in a soft voice, "They are students from school. They all came to get a ... Li'berry Fruit."

"What type of fruit?" Lyla's mom asked, puzzled. "I've never heard of such a strange-sounding fruit before in my life." She opened the gate wide enough for Lyla to pass through. "Why don't we go inside the house so you can tell me what's going on, young lady."

Mrs. Lyte scooped Joey up off the grass and

walked inside the house. Lyla followed closely behind. She knew trouble was coming her way.

"Now, what is this strange fruit you're talking about?" her mom asked.

"It's not actually a fruit," Lyla explained. "That's what Samantha, Megan, Nick, and I call the books that grew on the tree."

Lyla's mom's face became flushed. "Didn't we have a talk about keeping Li'berry Fruit, I mean books, a secret?"

"Megan told them," Lyla replied as a tear slowly trickled down her face. "It wasn't my fault."

Mrs. Lyte didn't want Lyla to start crying, so she decided not to drill her with any more questions. Instead, she wiped Lyla's tears away and calmly said, "No need to start crying. You can go and give them all a Li'berry Fruit."

"Thanks, Mom," Lyla said, sniffling. She darted back outside and opened the gate. All the children rushed in and packed around the tree house like sardines. It was as if they were giving away free candy.

"Promise me that once you all get your

Li'berry Fruit, you'll put them away in your cinch sacks," said Lyla.

All of the students nodded in agreement.

Lyla and the Troops formed an assembly line and started lugging handfuls of Li'berry Fruit down from the tree house. The eager readers were in such awe when they secured a Li'berry Fruit in their hands. They also did as they promised and placed their Li'berry Fruit in their cinch sacks. They were cheering as if they'd found gold.

As Lyla passed out Li'berry Fruit, she looked up and saw Mary Englemouth walking across the street with her head hung low. Lyla remembered seeing a Li'berry Fruit that Mary might enjoy reading.

She rushed inside and began searching. *I know it's here somewhere,* she said to herself.

As she continued to look, she noticed a pile of books. The one on top had a picture of an animal on the cover that she had never seen before. The hardcover book was titled *How to Clean a Hippopotamus.* As she picked it up, she thought, *Wow ... Joey's head is gigantic just like this baby hippopotamus's head.* She giggled to herself because, by combining "dent" and "hippopotamus," she just created a new name for her baby brother—*Dentopotamus!* Lyla glanced down at the rest of the stack and instantly found the Li'berry Fruit she wanted to give Mary Englemouth.

"Found it!" she said jubilantly. *And the character on the cover looks just like her!* she thought as she tucked the book under her arm.

"Lyla, what are you doing?" Samantha yelled from the base of the tree. She was still down there passing out Li'berry Fruit to a group of frantic children.

"I'm coming out right now," Lyla yelled back and climbed down from the tree house.

By the time Lyla caught up with her, Mary Englemouth had already reached the end of the block.

"Mary," Lyla called out. "I have something for you." She handed her the Li'berry Fruit.

Mary Englemouth took the book, looked at the cover and read aloud, *"Fancy Nancy Tea Party."*

"You look just like her," Lyla said. "And you

wear stuff in your hair and dazzling dresses … just like her."

Mary Englemouth cracked a smile. "Thanks!"

"You're welcome," Lyla responded with a smile.

"I'm sorry for calling you a dummy," Mary Englemouth said. "That wasn't nice of me."

"Friends?" Lyla offered, extending her hand.

Mary Englemouth shook Lyla's hand and said, "Friends." Then she walked away reading her Li'berry Fruit.

Who would have thought that Mary Englemouth and I would be friends? thought Lyla.

She turned back toward her house when she heard Nick yell, "READING TIME!"

Finally, all of the students departed, leaving the Troops in the backyard. As soon as Lyla returned, they retreated to the tree house.

"I'm sorry, Lyla," Megan said as they sat down with their Li'berry Fruit. "I know I can't keep my big mouth shut for nothing!"

"That's OK. I forgive you. Besides, we needed

to get rid of these books anyway," Lyla responded, giving Megan a big hug. "It sure got crowded with all of this Li'berry Fruit growing on the tree."

"Lyla," Samantha said, "how many Li'berries grow on the tree every morning?"

"Ummm," said Lyla, placing her finger against her temple. "I think around forty."

Samantha quickly started multiplying numbers in her head like her brain was a calculator.

"What is she doing?" Nick whispered to Lyla.

40 books × 7 days × 4 weeks =

"I don't know," Lyla whispered back. "She's so still ... maybe she's pretending to be a tree."

Then Samantha yelled, "That's it. The tree will grow one thousand one hundred twenty Li'berries each month."

"Wow!" exclaimed Lyla. "That's a lot of books! We are definitely going to have to keep them in my bedroom."

"How did you learn how to do that?" asked Megan. "That was amazing!"

"I guess by reading my math Li'berry Fruit." Samantha smiled and held her book up high. "I never knew I was such a mathematician."

Lyla said, "I'm noticing that once you read, you can do ANYTHING!"

"You sure can," Samantha said in agreement.

Lyla looked around the tree house and then began picking scattered books up off the floor. "Can you guys help me stack these over there in the corner?"

"Yeah," said everyone except Nick. His face was buried in his Li'berry Fruit. Both girls placed their books facedown on the table and started helping Lyla. Nick didn't budge at all. Nothing could take his attention away from reading.

"Nick!" Lyla yelled as she squatted down to pick up more books. He was oblivious to everything around him. "Nick!" Lyla yelled again.

When he didn't respond, she walked over to him and waved her hand in front of his face.

"Huh?" he responded, his eyes still glued to the pages.

"Stop reading and help us!" Lyla demanded as she tried to pull the book out of his hands.

Nick placed his finger between the pages. "STOP!" he said dramatically. "I'm going to lose my page."

"Just take a pencil and mark in your Li'berry Fruit where you stopped reading," Megan suggested.

Nick couldn't believe Megan suggested such a thing. "I'm not writing in my Li'berry Fruit!" Just then, a light bulb lit up above his head. "Mark ... ummm ... book. Maybe we should create a bookmark, so you don't have to lose your page when you take a break from reading."

Samantha laughed. "Another crazy idea of yours, Nick!"

"You guys thought *I* was crazy when I first told you about books," Lyla said in Nick's defense. "Now look who's reading them."

Samantha blushed with embarrassment because she knew Lyla was right. Nick looked at Lyla and smiled before he got up to start helping the girls stack the remaining Li'berries.

11

Inspired by the Past

"**H**oney ... I'm home," Mr. Lyte yelled happily as he entered the house. This was peculiar because he usually sounded tired and grumpy after a hard day at work. Mr. Lyte placed his briefcase on the plush carpet and called for everyone to meet him in the living room. He couldn't wait to tell his family the big news.

Mrs. Lyte walked into the room first. She was holding Joey, who was sucking his thumb.

"Hi, hun," she said, greeting him like she did every day. "How was work?"

"You will never guess what happened today," he said. "I have the best news."

Mrs. Lyte didn't want to destroy her husband's

surprise, but she absolutely had to tell him. "We have a problem," she said. "And you're not going to like it."

"What now?" Mr. Lyte asked, his smile disappearing as he sat down on the living room couch.

"The children in Lyla's class know about Li'berry Fruit."

"They know about what?" he asked, confused.

"Li'berry Fruit!" said Lyla's mom.

"And ... what does this bizarre-sounding fruit have to do with me?" Mr. Lyte asked.

Just then, it dawned on Mrs. Lyte that her husband didn't know the secret name.

"I'm sorry," she said. "Li'berry Fruit is the name Lyla and her friends came up with for the books, to keep them a secret."

"So you're saying her classmates know about the books growing on the tree?" he asked and stood up. "This can't be happening! Their secret name obviously isn't working. And how did all of this happen?"

"I'll allow your daughter to explain," Mrs. Lyte

responded before yelling, "LYLAAA!" loud enough for her daughter, who was upstairs in her bedroom, to hear.

Lyla slowly descended the stairs with a sullen expression plastered on her face. As soon as she saw her dad, she began explaining: "Megan was showing her Li'berry Fruit to everyone when I arrived at school today—"

"Mayor Crinkle is promoting me to be his Director of Marketing," Mr. Lyte said, interrupting his daughter's account of what happened at school. "I'm not going to let Li'berry Fruit, or books, mess up my promotion!"

"Congratulations, honey!" Lyla's mom cheered. "That IS a big surprise."

Lyla's dad turned to his wife and said, "It didn't happen yet, and I will not allow anything to get in the way of me being the new Director of Marketing." He turned his attention back to Lyla. "I'm calling someone to get rid of that tree."

"Nooo!" begged Lyla, looking at her mom to come to her defense. "Please don't! I'll do anything. I'll keep my room clean every single day!"

Mrs. Lyte said nothing.

He picked up the house phone and started dialing. He placed the phone to his ear, and while it was ringing, he said, "I have made my decision!"

Huge crocodile tears fell from Lyla's eyes.

"Lyl got in twouble," Joey teased.

"Be quiet, DENTOPOTAMUS!" Lyla said, lashing out at her little brother before she ran outside and climbed inside the tree house.

"She'll be OK," Mrs. Lyte told her husband.

"This is the best thing for all of us," he responded.

Inside the tree house, Lyla dried her eyes, pushed a branch to the side and looked out the window.

"I guess this is good-bye forever," she said aloud as she looked at the tree. "The people of Screenfield are better off watching CrinkleTube. Children don't need to have fun learning," she said, trying to convince herself it was true.

Suddenly, a book fell from one of the branches. *THUMP!*

Lyla quickly turned and tilted her head

downward. *I thought we knocked down all of the books this morning.*

She walked over to the book, squatted and picked it up. On the cover was a picture of a petite, older lady in the forest. She wore a patterned scarf on her head, a long-sleeve shirt, and a long skirt. Lyla read the title aloud, "*The Story of Harriet Tubman.*" *Who is she?* Lyla wondered. *I've never heard of her before.*

Curious, Lyla sat down and opened the book. With every page, she became **Inspired by the Past**. She related her dilemma to Harriet's. Just as the people depended on Harriet for a better life, Lyla knew the people of Screenfield counted on her. *If Harriet can fight for her people, I can too,* she thought, completely encouraged after reading the book.

Lyla had a new mission. She was recommitted to freeing the people of Screenfield from CrinkleTube, and she was not going to give up this time. Lyla slammed the book shut, stood up proudly and declared, "I shall lead my people to READOM! Hey, I did it. I used my imagination.

Readom means the freedom to read. Now that's a cool word!"

All of a sudden, a loud buzzing noise caught Lyla's attention. She walked over to the window and saw a tall man wearing green overalls that read *Be Gone Tree Removal Co.* on the back. In his hand, he held a shiny steel chainsaw that he was about to place against the tree trunk.

"STOP!" Lyla screamed from her tree house window, but the sound of the chainsaw overpowered her voice. "I said stop!" she yelled louder, but she was still unable to get the man's attention.

Lyla turned and dashed from her spot, climbed down the planks of the tree house and ran to her dad, who was watching. She tugged on his suit jacket to get his attention.

As soon as the man placed the teeth of the chainsaw against the tree trunk, billows of black-gray smoke began to rise, and the motor of the heavy machine sounded like it was dying. He immediately turned it off, removed his protective goggles, and took a look at the chainsaw to find that the teeth were all battered.

"What type of crazy tree is this?" he asked Mr. Lyte, puzzled.

"Why?" Mr. Lyte asked. He was standing a few feet away from the tree and didn't see what had happened.

"'Cause it ruined my chainsaw!" bellowed the man in the green overalls.

Mr. Lyte walked over to the tree and took a closer look. "Your chainsaw didn't scar the tree at all," he said in amazement.

Lyla smiled. Now she *knew* the tree was magical.

"I'm not going to let a tree beat me," declared the man. He walked to his red pickup truck, which was filled with landscaping tools he had thrown in back of the bed.

"Everyone, get out of the way!" he said.

Both Lyla and her dad moved back a few feet, closer to the porch.

The man hopped in his truck and started it. After revving up the engine, he backed the truck close to the gate, shifted the car into park, and then got out with the motor still running. He took a long, rusty chain from the bed and wrapped it around the tree trunk and the fender of his truck.

"We'll see who's the boss!" he declared.

He got back behind the wheel and stomped on the gas pedal. The truck tires spun in place. Then, without warning, the chain pulled the fender right off his truck. He slammed on the brakes, got out, and saw his fender on the ground. The tree was champ.

"Someone owes me for the damage to my truck and chainsaw!" the man in the green overalls said angrily.

Lyla and her dad looked at each other and chuckled. Mr. Lyte pulled his wallet out of his back pocket and paid the man eighty dollars. He collected his busted chainsaw and fender and threw them in the back of his truck before he drove off fuming.

"I guess Li'berry Fruit were meant to be," Lyla's dad said, looking down at his daughter and giving her a wink.

Lyla jumped up with glee and gave her dad a huge hug.

Mrs. Lyte came out of the house holding Dentopotamus. "What happened?" she asked. "What was that racket about?"

"I'm sorry, Mom," Lyla said.

The Lytes were baffled. "Sorry for what?" they asked in unison.

"I took the picture of Grandma reading the book to you without asking," Lyla confessed. "And I told my friends the secret about the buried books even though you told me not to."

Mrs. Lyte reached over and kissed Lyla on the forehead and said, "Everyone makes mistakes."

"The most important thing is that you apologized," Mr. Lyte added. "And you won't make the same mistakes again."

"I sure won't," Lyla responded. Then she tugged on her brother's bare foot. "And I'm sorry

for yelling at you, Dentopotamus."
Everyone laughed!

12

A Change for Once

The next morning, Lyla woke up determined that everyone in Screenfield have a Li'berry Fruit in their possession. All night she thought about how Harriet Tubman secretly went on her journey using the Underground Railroad. Lyla couldn't go on her mission late at night, and there was no underground anything in Screenfield, but she could get it done in the morning, prior to the start of school. And this time she would target both children and adults.

After Lyla and her dad finished their routine of removing all the books from the tree and storing them in the tree house, she secretly packed her cinch sack full of books and told her parents, "I'll walk to school this morning."

"Are you sure you don't want me to drop you at school?" Mr. Lyte asked.

"I'm sure," Lyla answered and grabbed her brown-bag lunch from her mom. "You'll only make me late, and today is a new day for me."

"My baby is growing up," Lyla's mom said, pinching her rosy cheeks.

"Mom," Lyla said as she pulled away. "You're embarrassing me."

"You be careful walking to school," her dad said. "And have a great day!"

"OK!" Lyla responded as she rushed out the front door.

Lyla's first stop was Crinkle Cuts. She felt that there was more to hair than just a simple, boring short Afro. She liked Nick and her dad's haircut, but in her opinion they needed to rock something different. They needed a new style. Crinkle Cut's mailbox was on the front door of the shop. The first thing the owner, Mrs. Tanya Shavers, did before opening the shop was go through her mail. Lyla slipped a Li'berry Fruit into the slot and hurried off to her second destination.

Next was her favorite restaurant in Screenfield, Dish Dining. They wouldn't be open until lunchtime. The restaurant only served one type of sandwich for lunch—sliced turkey on a submarine bun with all the fixings (lettuce, tomatoes, mustard, and pickles). The sandwich was yummy, but ordering the exact same meal every day would drive anyone insane. Dinner there was not much better. Cheese pizza was their signature—and only—dish. They made thin crust, stuffed and deep-dish cheese pizzas, but no matter how much they dressed it up, it tasted the exact same: cheese on top of baked dough.

There was no mail slot on the front door, only a handwritten sign that read: *All Deliveries Made in the Back.* Lyla walked around to the rear of the restaurant and saw a stack of pizza boxes at the door. She placed the Li'berry Fruit on the top box and rushed off.

I'd better hurry up before I'm late for school, Lyla thought. *I only have two stops left. If I'm going to have everyone in Screenfield reading books, I'd better recruit the Troops to help me.*

Lyla successfully dropped a Li'berry Fruit in all her planned locations and arrived at school right before the bell rang. At recess, she met with the Troops. She didn't have to convince them to help her because they all agreed that getting everyone in Screenfield to read Li'berries was most important.

Weeks passed and the Troops had secretly placed books in the mailboxes of businesses and homes around town. There was **A Change for Once** spreading throughout Screenfield. Children discovered the wonderful world of make-believe, and their imaginations grew wings. Backyards were filled with pirates scavenging for hidden treasures. Little girls' bedrooms became castles where they waited for their Prince Charming to save them from the fire-breathing dragon. Li'berry Fruit inspired children to read, draw, paint, and even write their own stories.

Even Lyla's mom was reading. She had grown attached to a few ABC children's picture books that she read to Dentopotamus every day, which helped him pronounce Lyla's name correctly. Her mom was also reading gardening books, which she used to help her create an oasis of daffodils, lilies, petunias, marigolds, daisies, and a rainbow of roses (Lyla's favorite) in the backyard.

Mrs. Shavers learned how to do different hairstyles after she read her Li'berry Fruit. Lyla's dad now rocked a fade, while Nick rocked a

Mohawk, which was the new hairstyle all the boys were rocking in Screenfield. Mrs. Shavers changed her shop's name to Crinkle Styles.

While on one morning mission, Nick asked Lyla, "Did you know Dish Dining serves all types of meals now?"

"Hey, that's magnificent!" Lyla exclaimed. "Their Li'berry Fruit must have helped them too. It taught them how to cook a variety of foods."

"Wow, Lyla! You're using words I've never heard before," Nick said.

"What do you mean?" Lyla asked.

"Like the word va-ri-e-ty," Nick replied.

"Oh ... that word," said Lyla. "I read it in a book yesterday. It means to have different types of things."

"I get it!" Nick exclaimed, beaming because he expanded his vocabulary. "That's why they now have menus. They serve a *variety* of dishes for breakfast, lunch, and dinner."

Lyla gave Nick a thumbs-up. She was ecstatic to see everyone learning new things by reading. Even Megan started a dance club where she taught students ballet. And each day after school, a group of children followed Lyla home like a herd of sheep following their shepherd.

Happiness infected everyone in Screenfield, except for one person—Mayor Crinkle!

"Mrs. Holmes, get in my office!" yelled an angry Mayor Crinkle. "Now!"

"Did I do something wrong, sir?" Mrs. Holmes asked as she sat down.

With a loud voice, Mayor Crinkle began, "CrinkleTube's ratings are plummeting." He pounded his fist on his desk, almost putting a dent in it. "What is occupying the people of this town so much that they don't have time to watch CrinkleTube?"

"I don't know," Mrs. Holmes answered promptly.

Mayor Crinkle did not like that answer one bit. His face became more flushed, and the wrinkles on his faced deepened.

"What do you mean *you don't know*?" He shouted. "I pay you to know what I don't know. Whatever I don't know, you need to know, so I can know."

"Maybe ... everyone's tubevision is broken?" Mrs. Holmes innocently guessed. "And that's causing the viewer ratings to plunge."

Mayor Crinkle had a serious look on his face. "Was that a joke, Mrs. Holmes?"

"No," she replied. "Not at all."

"I have a joke," Mayor Crinkle said sarcastically. "Knock, knock."

"Who's there?"

"You are."

"You are who?"

"You are fired ... if you don't find out why people aren't watching CrinkleTube!" he shouted.

Mrs. Holmes was so startled by his words that she fell backward and rolled out of her chair.

"Now get up and go do some spying!" Mayor Crinkle ordered and pointed to the door.

Mrs. Holmes picked herself up off the floor and left, nervous about getting fired. She exited

City Hall, squeezed into her compact Beetle, and drove around Screenfield looking for anything out of the ordinary. Nothing caught her watchful eye, so she decided to park her car and walk around to find out what was going on. As she strolled through the neighborhood, she saw children having fun in their backyards.

That's weird, she thought. *Children enjoying themselves without watching CrinkleTube ... There's definitely something bizarre happening in this town.*

Suddenly, from a distance, Mrs. Holmes saw a long line of children in Lyla's backyard.

"If I'm going to get to the bottom of this, I've got to figure out what's going on and who lives there. I don't want them to see me," Mrs. Holmes muttered to herself.

She squatted down and hid behind the bushes closest to Lyla's house. Then, she crouched from bush to bush until she was close enough to see what was happening. Children's voices grew louder the closer she slithered. She knew she was near the line because she could clearly hear what they were discussing.

"I love my Li'berry Fruit!" said a little girl with a high-pitched voice.

"Meee tooo," agreed a little boy who sang his words as he spoke.

"Li'berry Fruit is the best!" said a third boyish voice. "It's way better than tubevision."

In the tree house, Megan handed Nick more Li'berries. Then he tossed them down to Samantha, who waited at the foot of the tree house. When she caught a Li'berry Fruit, she gave it to Lyla to pass out.

"Can I get one tomorrow when I finish this one?" asked the girl with the high-pitched voice.

"Of course," Lyla answered cheerfully. "There is an abundance to go around."

"So ... that's what's keeping everyone from watching CrinkleTube," Mrs. Holmes murmured. "Li'berry Fruit."

"Thank you," the girl said when she received her Li'berry Fruit. "See you tomorrow after school."

Behind the bushes, Mrs. Holmes was having a difficult time. "OUCH! Why are these bushes so prickly?" she muttered to herself. And, to make it worse, she completely forgot that she was allergic to bushes. "ACHOOO!"

"Samantha, did you hear a sneeze coming from those bushes?" Lyla asked, startled.

"I did," confirmed Samantha, who was just as startled.

"Maybe we should go take a look!" Lyla

insisted as she tugged Samantha by the arm. "I think it's coming from over there."

Mrs. Holmes heard Lyla and Samantha rustling through the bushes. *Oh no!* she thought. *Now I have two things to worry about. One, I'm going to get caught spying on them, and two, Mayor Crinkle is going to fire me!* Then an idea popped into her head. *I'll act like I'm looking for something that I lost ... but what?"*

As soon as the Troops got closer to Mrs. Holmes' hiding place, she jumped up and wiped dirt and broken branches off her pants.

"Mrs. Holmes! What are you doing in the bushes?" Lyla asked, shocked.

"I'm looking for my ... ummm." Then, it finally hit her. "Dog ... yeah ... my dog!"

"What's your dog's name?" Samantha asked.

"Uhmmm ... Spot," she replied. "His name is Spot."

Lyla glanced at Samantha suspiciously and squinted her eyes. She'd never heard of Mrs. Holmes having a dog. "What does Spot look like?" Lyla asked.

"He has a tail and four legs," Mrs. Holmes said, slowly moving backward.

"Don't all dogs look like that?" Samantha asked.

"So ... you shouldn't have any problems finding him," said Mrs. Holmes as she quickly turned and scurried away. "Thank you ... Bye."

13

The Report

Mrs. Holmes returned to City Hall bursting with good news. "Can you tell Mayor Crinkle that I'm here to see him?" she asked Ms. Weatherspoon.

"OK," Ms. Weatherspoon said. She called Mayor Crinkle, and he instructed her to show Mrs. Holmes into his office suite.

"So, what did you find?" Mayor Crinkle asked. He was sitting in his huge chair with his back to her.

"I know why people are not watching CrinkleTube anymore," Mrs. Holmes said confidently.

Mayor Crinkle slowly swirled around in his chair. "So ... let me hear **The Report**."

She began to explain, "It has to do with Li'berry Fruit. Everyone in town is talking about them."

"LI'BERRY FRUIT!" said Mayor Crinkle, irritated. "All you brought back was an idiotic name of a fruit!"

Mrs. Holmes grew more nervous, and sweat dripped down her forehead. "Yes ... I did."

"So ... you're telling me my viewer ratings are in the toilet due to Li'berry Fruit?" Mayor Crinkle asked.

Mrs. Holmes took a deep breath and looked Mayor Crinkle straight in the eye. "That's the reason ... sir."

"Well, I choose not to believe that is the foolish reason why people are not watching CrinkleTube," he said angrily. "You wasted my time, and I refuse to waste any more tax dollars paying your salary."

"Give me a little more time," Mrs. Holmes begged. "I promise I will bring back a better reason."

"Your time is up," Mayor Crinkle screamed as

he stood up. "You are FIRED!" He hit his balled fist on the desk. "And that's not a joke."

Mrs. Holmes walked to the door and opened it. Suddenly, she stopped and looked back at the mayor. "I've wanted to say this for the longest time."

"What?" Mayor Crinkle asked sarcastically.

"You are the worst mayor Screenfield has ever seen!" she snapped.

Mrs. Holmes comment did not phase Mayor Crinkle at all. "Thank you for that compliment," he said, grinning. "But please don't go away mad … Just go away!"

Mrs. Holmes left and slammed the door behind her.

Mayor Crinkle rushed to the door, opened it and bellowed, "I guess I have to do this job myself!" Then, he turned his attention to Ms. Weatherspoon, who was sitting at her desk. "Where's Mr. Lyte?"

"He took off work today, sir," replied Ms. Weatherspoon.

Mayor Crinkle began walking toward the taping room. "Follow me," he ordered. "Today is your lucky day."

"It is?" Ms. Weatherspoon jumped up out of her seat. "How?"

"You have just been promoted to Mr. Lyte's position," Mayor Crinkle said with a smirk. "You are the new camera operator for CrinkleTube. We are going on the air with News Watch in two minutes."

"Thank you for the opportunity, sir," said a jittery Ms. Weatherspoon. "But I don't know how to work a camera. I might break it."

Mayor Crinkle sat in front of the camera at the news desk. He adjusted his tie, which was green with white polka dots. "How hard can it be to operate a camera? All you do is get behind it and press record while I'm giving the news report."

"Well, I guess I can," said Ms. Weatherspoon as she positioned herself behind the huge camera and aimed it right at Mayor Crinkle's face.

"I'm ready to go," he said.

"Three ... two ... one ... You're on the air, sir," Ms. Weatherspoon said, cuing Mayor Crinkle. On the monitor, he was upside down, but Ms. Weatherspoon said nothing and proceeded with the live broadcast of the news.

"People of Screenfield," began Mayor Crinkle. "This is a special news report. Matter of fact, this is an emergency news report! Actually, this is a special emergency news report!" he said in a gruff tone. "If anyone, that means *everyone* living in

173

Screenfield, is caught doing anything else for entertainment other than watching CrinkleTube, you will be thrown in jail."

Unfortunately, no one in Screenfield saw the news that day because their tubevisions were turned off. Mayor Crinkle did not notice that the viewer rating was zero. There was no need to watch CrinkleTube anymore. Everyone was occupied and having fun reading Li'berries.

When he was finished, Mayor Crinkle removed his glasses and said, "Now call my driver and tell him to put my shiny red ax in the trunk." *If Li'berry Fruit does exist, then there must be a tree,* he thought to himself. *And I'm going to chop it down.*

"OK, sir," Ms. Weatherspoon said. Once she got to her desk, she pressed the big, red intercom button to call his driver.

"Yes," Mr. Butler answered over the speaker.

"Bring the limo around and put Mayor Crinkle's ax in the trunk," directed Ms. Weatherspoon.

"I'm on my way," Mr. Butler replied.

When Mr. Butler pulled up in the circular driveway in the black stretch limo, he honked the horn. Mayor Crinkle ran out of the front door of City Hall and jumped in. The dark tinted window separating the driver from the backseat automatically rolled down.

"Where to, sir?" Mr. Butler asked.

"Just drive," Mayor Crinkle ordered harshly.

As Mr. Butler drove, Mayor Crinkle looked out of his window to see what people in Screenfield were doing. He rolled his tinted window down to get a better look.

"Why aren't these people inside their houses watching CrinkleTube?" Mayor Crinkle wondered aloud. "And what type of ridiculous hairstyles are the boys wearing?"

"It looks like everyone is having fun outside," Mr. Butler said. "And I kind of like their haircuts. I should get mine cut the same way."

"I didn't ask you," Mayor Crinkle said with a harsh tone. "I pay you to drive ... not to talk."

The limo stopped at the stop light at the

intersection of Ratings Road and Antenna Avenue. Mayor Crinkle overheard two boys with high Mohawks talking while waiting to cross the street.

"Look, I'm a football player," pretended David Danielson, as he tucked his Li'berry Fruit in his sweaty armpit. He was the bigger of the two boys, and he loved imagining he was a great running back.

"Your Li'berry Fruit is better than mine," said Montez Gonzales, who was smaller than David.

The traffic light turned green, and Mr. Butler punched the gas pedal.

"STOP the limo!" Mayor Crinkle yelled, frightening Mr. Butler. The limo came to a sudden halt, bouncing Mayor Crinkle around in the back. He opened the door and ran over to the boys.

"Did I hear one of you say you have a Li'berry Fruit?" he asked.

Both boys jumped back.

"Who are you?" asked David, squeezing his arm down tight to fully conceal his Li'berry Fruit.

"I am the mayor of this town," Mayor Crinkle replied, not noticing the book. "So let me see your Li'berry Fruit."

"No, you're not the mayor!" Montez exclaimed.

"Yes, I certainly am," Mayor Crinkle retorted.

"Well, if you are, then prove it," said Montez.

The first thing that came to Mayor Crinkle's mind was his Crinkle Academy morning song. "I'll sing my Good Morning song for you."

He sang no more than five seconds of the song before David yelled, "That's enough! Stop with that awful wailing!" (Wailing was a new word he had learned from reading his Li'berry Fruit.)

"Yeah, you're hurting my eardrums!" Montez agreed, covering his ears. "You're our mayor all right."

"You sure look skinnier on tubevision," David said, eyeing Mayor Crinkle up and down.

"Again, let me see your Li'berry Fruit!" commanded Mayor Crinkle, ignoring their assessment of him. "You little brats!"

Suddenly, Montez kicked Mayor Crinkle in the shin.

"OUCH!" Mayor Crinkle yelped, jumping on one leg while holding the other one. "I meant to say 'little boys,'" he said, still wincing at the pain in his shin.

"We'll let you see it if you give us five dollars," David said with a smirk.

"OK, OK," Mayor Crinkle said as he pulled a crisp five-dollar bill out of his pocket and handed it to him.

Montez grabbed the money, looked at David and said, "Give it to him."

"Why do I have to give him my Li'berry Fruit?" David asked, pouting. "Give him yours."

"No. I just got mine today," said Montez, tightly gripping his cinch sack.

"Fine," David agreed. "I get most of the money then!" He removed his Li'berry Fruit from his armpit and handed it to the mayor.

Mayor Crinkle's eyes nearly bulged out of his head when he saw what the boys had called Li'berry Fruit.

"This isn't fruit ... It's a BOOK!" he shouted furiously. "So, everyone in Screenfield is reading. I will put a stop to this. They will not have books in my town!"

The two boys were bickering over the money.

"Let me hold it," demanded David as he clutched the bill.

"I was the one who got it," said Montez.

A very irritated Mayor Crinkle interrupted their argument. "I have had a sudden change of heart," he said and snatched the five-dollar bill out of their hands and jumped into the limo with the book. "Mr. Butler, drive!"

14

A Lot Better

"How did these books reappear?" asked Mayor Crinkle, dumbfounded. "I buried them decades ago."

"Boss, look over there," Mr. Butler said and pointed as they passed by Lyla's house.

They saw loads of children in Lyla's backyard waiting to receive a Li'berry Fruit. Mayor Crinkle looked closely and saw books being handed from one child to another.

"Turn this limo around, instantly!" he commanded.

Mr. Butler abruptly whipped the car into a U-turn, causing Mayor Crinkle to slide to the opposite side of the backseat. Then, he stopped at the red traffic light at Remote Road and Crinkle Street.

"What are you doing?" Mayor Crinkle asked harshly.

"The light is red, sir," Mr. Butler replied calmly.

"I don't have time to sit here and wait," the mayor shouted. "Drive, you idiot!"

"But," said Mr. Butler.

"Don't but me! I said drive!" a very angry Mayor Crinkle ordered.

Mr. Butler punched the gas pedal and proceeded through the red light.

Officer Jerry Gilbert, who was sitting at the traffic light, turned on his siren and began chasing the speeding limo.

"Don't stop until you reach that house filled with all of those brats and books," instructed Mayor Crinkle.

"OK," Mr. Butler replied, ignoring the siren and Officer Gilbert's bright red lights.

The limo and the squad car pulled into the Lytes' driveway at the same time. The wailing sound of the siren brought Lyla's mom, dad, and all of the neighbors to the front yard. They were met by Mayor Crinkle, who flew out of the limo.

"FREEZE!" yelled Officer Gilbert.

Mayor Crinkle stopped dead in his tracks, raised his hands high in the air, and slowly turned to face the officer.

"Oh, it's our mayor," Officer Gilbert said, relaxing a bit. "Sorry about that, sir."

"You should be sorry," said Mayor Crinkle.

"But I must say, sir," Officer Gilbert began, "you look a lot thinner on tubevision."

Lyla's dad panicked when he saw his boss standing in his front yard. He knew it was only a matter of time before the mayor saw the books and fired him as a result.

"What brings you out here, Mayor?" he asked, trying to sound nonchalant.

Mayor Crinkle ignored Mr. Lyte's question. His eyes surveyed the Lytes' property. "Is this your house?" he asked.

"Yes, it is," Mr. Lyte answered, his voice cracking.

"And are you allowing this to go on here?" asked Mayor Crinkle.

Mr. Lyte shrugged his shoulders. "Allowing

what to go on?"

"Passing out Li'berry Fruit, I mean books, to children," Mayor Crinkle responded.

Mr. Lyte paused and looked around at all the children holding books. They all had huge smiles on their faces as they sat around the Lytes' yard reading. "But they're helping children learn," he said.

"Crinkle Academy is all they need to learn," Mayor Crinkle argued angrily.

Lyla, who was listening to their conversation, stopped passing out Li'berries and ran over to her dad. "CrinkleTube is boring!" she said, interrupting the two men. "Children would rather read a Li'berry Fruit."

The crowd supported Lyla with cheers.

"And who are you?" asked a more frustrated Mayor Crinkle as his eyes locked on Lyla.

"I'm the girl who found the seed ... that grew into a tree ... that blossomed into books," Lyla answered proudly.

"Mr. Lyte," said Mayor Crinkle. "I take it that this is your little brat?"

Lyla's dad was offended. "She's not a brat," he stated as he pulled Lyla closer to him. "She's my daughter."

"This is my town, and I'll say what's boring and what's not," Mayor Crinkle yelled.

Lyla's mom interrupted, "Excuse me, Mayor Crinkle, but this is everybody's town."

"Mr. Lyte, I need you to put an end to this nonsense!" Mayor Crinkle said. "Do you want your new, high-paying position, or do you want to pass out books for the rest of your life?"

Before Lyla's dad could answer, Lyla darted inside the tree house.

"What is she going to do?" asked people in the crowd. Even her parents didn't know.

She returned holding a sheet of paper. "Here, Mom and Dad," Lyla said, handing it to them to read.

Mrs. Lyte looked on as Mr. Lyte read for everyone to hear:

Room 201

Writing

<u>What I Love About Screenfield</u>

Screenfield is a wonderful and magical place where anything can happen. It's vivid like the colors of a children's picture book. It's where children read all day in the bright, yellow sun and into the warm, welcoming night.

In Screenfield, children's imaginations emerge when they open fantastic books, and their dreams dance on dazzling stars.

In Screenfield, friends attach to you like luscious green leaves on a tall tree. Through thick and thin, no matter what, friendships blossom like beautiful yellow tulips.

In Screenfield, I love my enormous tree house, the marvelous restaurant, the stupendous hair shop, and the fabulous people. Everyone in Screenfield is unique in their own special way.

Best of all, I love my family in Screenfield. My mom and dad support me and help me with whatever I do, from comforting me when I got an *F* on my essay, to having a positive attitude about me finding a strange seed.

My parents are my superheroes, and they always make me feel like a pretty princess. And, not to leave out my baby brother, Joey "Dentopotamus" is a perfect prince in the making.

There's no better place in the entire world than the home of Li'berry Fruit, where books actually grow on a tree, like fruit.

When Lyla's dad finished reading her revised writing assignment, the Troops huddled around her, hugging and patting her on the back.

"Lyla, you can write!" Samantha said excitedly.

"That's the best paper I've ever heard anyone write!" Nick praised.

"I loved all those big words you used," added Megan.

"I think I'm going to cry," Lyla's mom said with a sniffle. "That paper was ... **A Lot Better!**"

Lyla's dad was puzzled. "How did your writing improve so fast?" he asked.

"Ever since the tree grew books," Lyla began, "I have been an avid reader." She lightly touched the side of her head with her finger and said, "I'm now able to USE my imagination."

"I'm very proud of you," Lyla's mom told her. "You never stopped until you became a better writer."

"Me too!" her dad said, giving her a side hug.

"We three," added the Troops.

"Enough of the pathetic family moment," interrupted Mayor Crinkle, fuming. "One more chance, Mr. Lyte. Is it going to be CrinkleTube or those useless books?"

15

The Last Chapter

"I QUIT!" Lyla's dad said to Mayor Crinkle. "I'm done working for you."

The crowd cheered ecstatically.

Mayor Crinkle was traumatized. He couldn't believe that one of his employees actually quit on him ... *before* he had a chance to fire him. "You have made the worst decision of your life!" he said furiously.

"And another thing," Lyla's dad added joyfully. "I have some magnificent news of my own."

"What is it?" Lyla asked curiously.

"I've been reading my own Li'berry Fruit," he said proudly as he pulled a book out of his back pocket. "I'm learning how to fix cars, and I'm opening Lyte's Car Repair Shop."

190

"You can start by fixing my truck," offered the man in the green overalls from the crowd.

"Are you sure you are making the right decision?" Mrs. Lyte asked.

"This is the best decision I've ever made in my entire life," he said with a confident smile.

Lyla was ecstatic. "Dad, you have been reading books all this time? That's great!"

Mr. Lyte's eyes dropped as he looked at his daughter and said, "You made me remember how much fun reading is. Because of you, I have a love for reading again."

"That goes for me too," added her mom. "My little princess!"

"Awww!" exclaimed Lyla. "I have the utmost greatest ... spectacular ... incomparably astonishing parents ever—"

"We get the picture," interrupted her dad.

"This is **The Last Chapter** for you and those books," Mayor Crinkle threatened, pointing at Lyla's dad. "Driver, give me my tool."

Mr. Butler opened the trunk of the limo and pulled out the huge ax. The crowd gasped as he handed it to Mayor Crinkle.

"I'll show all of you who makes the decisions in this town," Mayor Crinkle declared. He waved the ax in the air as he walked over to the tree.

"I wouldn't do that if I were you," the man in the green overalls warned.

Mayor Crinkle ignored him and swung the ax at the fattest part of the tree. As soon as the ax hit the tree, it bounced off and flew out of his hands. It twirled as it rose higher in the air. As quickly as the deadly ax rose in the sky, it began to fall, heading directly for the top of Lyla's head.

"I'll save you," Nick shouted. With lightning fast speed, he ran toward Lyla and pushed her out of the way.

The ax landed with a thud right into the ground where Lyla had stood.

"Nick, you saved my life," Lyla said, breathless.

Samantha and Megan ran over to help her up.

"Good job, Nick," Mr. Lyte said, walking over and patting him on his shoulder.

Nick quickly ripped off his shirt and snap-on jogging pants.

"You can call me SUPER NICK," he shouted gleefully, standing in red underwear with a red sheet tied around his neck. On his white T-shirt were the letters SN, written in bright red marker.

Mayor Crinkle stood there frozen in shock. He wanted the troublemakers thrown in jail.

"Arrest the entire Lyte family!" he bellowed to Officer Gilbert.

Officer Gilbert did not move. "They are not breaking any laws," he stated calmly.

"I beg to differ," Mayor Crinkle responded.

Then, like a firecracker, he exploded. "They are breaking Screenfield's No Reading Books Law, and I want those perpetrators arrested and thrown in jail!"

Officer Gilbert still didn't budge.

"I gave you an order as mayor of Screenfield," declared Mayor Crinkle. "Now go do your job!"

Officer Gilbert began walking slowly toward the Lyte family. Lyla leaned against her dad, afraid of what was about to happen.

"That's like a good officer," Mayor Crinkle muttered under his breath.

Officer Gilbert stopped in front of Lyla's dad, reached his hand out and grabbed the book Mr. Lyte was holding. "So this is what they call a Li'berry Fruit?" he asked as he held it in his hand.

"Don't you dare join the ranks of those perpetrators," commanded Mayor Crinkle.

Officer Gilbert ignored the mayor, opened the book, and started to read. Within seconds, a gigantic smile lit up his face.

"Put down that book and do your job!" commanded Mayor Crinkle.

Officer Gilbert closed the book, turned toward Mayor Crinkle and said, "Arresting them would be wrong. Li'berry Fruit is the best thing that has ever happened to Screenfield." He turned to look at all the children reading books and playing. "Look around," he continued. "The children are happy. It takes a courageous child to do what this little girl did."

Lyla looked up, beaming at Officer Gilbert.

"I'll show you who's brave," bellowed Mayor Crinkle as he ran full throttle toward Officer Gilbert. "Give me that book!"

"No!" replied Officer Gilbert, grasping the book tighter.

"I said give it to me!" shouted Mayor Crinkle.

They tugged and tugged back and forth.

"Let it go!" demanded Officer Gilbert.

Mayor Crinkle pulled with a final, hard yank. His grip became loose and he fell backward into the tree, hitting his head and landing on his butt.

BANG! The tree swayed and a book fell out of the tree hitting Mayor Crinkle on top of his bald head. It landed right in his lap.

Mayor Crinkle shook the dizziness off and looked down at the hard cover of the book. *"Become a Better You,"* he said, reading the title to himself. Then, he couldn't resist opening the book. The words touched his heart and soul instantly, and he sat there for twenty minutes reading in amazement.

Lyla walked up to him, knelt, and tapped him on his shoulder. "Are you OK?" she asked.

Mayor Crinkle looked up at her and smiled. "I've never felt better in my whole life!" he replied as he stood up.

With the book in his hand, Mayor Crinkle marched to the top of the Lytes' front porch.

He glanced at the book, and then at the crowd. "People of Screenfield, gather around," Mayor Crinkle directed loudly.

The crowd was baffled. They didn't know what Mayor Crinkle was going to do or say next.

He took a deep breath and exhaled. "I have not been the best person, or mayor, in Screenfield," he declared.

"Yeah, he's right," the crowd said in agreement.

"Is that our mayor?" Nick whispered to the Troops.

"It looks like him," Samantha answered.

"But it doesn't sound like him," Megan added.

Mayor Crinkle continued, "I'm sorry for not allowing you to read books. I should never have placed a cage around your imaginations."

"Dad," Lyla whispered to her father, "Mayor Crinkled changed."

"For the better," replied Mr. Lyte.

Mayor Crinkle held up the book. "As of today, everyone is allowed to READ BOOKS!"

All of the people in the town jumped up and down, cheering, "Mayor ... Mayor ... Mayor!"

Mayor Crinkle held his hand up and the crowd became quiet. "I am also changing the town's name back to what it was originally—Coverfield!"

"Hurray, Hurray!" everyone shouted.

In the midst of the celebration, Lyla walked up the steps and yanked on Mayor Crinkle's suit jacket. He bent his bald head down, and Lyla whispered into his ear.

Mayor Crinkle gave her a thumbs-up, straightened and said, "Of course I can grant that wish."

Lyla beamed from ear to ear.

"Citizens of Coverfield, I have more great

news," said Mayor Crinkle, looking into the sea of people. "We will build Coverfield a new li'berry to house all of the books growing on that wonderful tree."

Everyone welcomed the terrific news with applause.

Lyla tugged on Mayor Crinkle's suit jacket once more. He crouched and she whispered into his ear again.

Afterward, he straightened up. "I mean LIBRARY," he corrected himself, smiling.

The crowd was exuberant. Everyone cheered, "Hip-hip-hurray! Hip-hip-hurray!"

Mayor Crinkle knelt down to Lyla's level. "Thank you for not giving up," he said. "Because of you, everyone will be able to use their imaginations and have fun reading books. You made life in Coverfield a lot better." Then, he gave Lyla a big hug.

Lyla was all smiles. She ran down the steps to her mom and said, "See ... some dreams DO come TRUE!"

Lyla Lyte and the Li'berry Fruit